Imaginalis

Imaginalis

J. M. DeMATTEIS

KATHERINE TEGEN BOOKS

An Imprint of HarperCollins*Publishers*

Katherine Tegen Books is an imprint of HarperCollins Publishers.

Imaginalis
Copyright © 2010 by J. M. DeMatteis

Library of Congress Cataloging-in-Publication Data
DeMatteis, J. M.
Imaginalis / J. M. DeMatteis. — 1st ed.
p. cm.
Summary: Devastated that her favorite fantasy book series will not
be completed, twelve-year-old Mehera discovers that only her belief,
imagination, and courage will save the land of Imaginalis and its
inhabitants from being lost forever.
ISBN 978-0-06-173286-7 (trade bdg.)
[1. Books and reading—Fiction. 2. Imagination—Fiction.
3. Magic—Fiction. 4. Fathers and daughters—Fiction. 5. Middle
schools—Fiction. 6. Schools—Fiction.] I. Title.
PZ7.D3916Im 2010   2009039764
[Fic]—dc22   CIP
                                                               AC

Typography by Amy Ryan
10 11 12 13 14   CG/RRDB   10 9 8 7 6 5 4 3 2 1
❖
First Edition

For Diane, Cody, and Katie—
whose love keeps me tethered
while I sail across the universes

Thanks to Molly O'Neill for her editorial acumen, Brendan Deneen for watching my back, and Irv and Rosalie Epstein for their constant support.

Special thanks to Brenda Bowen, who made this book possible; and, as always, to the Dreamer of dreamers, Avatar Meher Baba.

TABLE OF CONTENTS

Prologue:	*A Beginning*	1
Chapter One	*Another Beginning*	3
Chapter Two	*Celeste's Opinion*	17
Chapter Three	*An Ending*	23
Chapter Four	*Shock*	30
Chapter Five	*Dear Mrs. Morice-Gilland*	34
Chapter Six	*Come Back*	43
Chapter Seven	*Contact*	51
Chapter Eight	*The Cocoon*	58
Chapter Nine	*The Elephant*	63
Chapter Ten	*The Choice*	72
Chapter Eleven	*Across the Unbelievable Bridge*	80
Chapter Twelve	*Nolandia*	86
Chapter Thirteen	*A Song of Hope*	94

Chapter Fourteen	*The Escape*	105
Chapter Fifteen	*The New World*	111
Chapter Sixteen	*Visions*	121
Chapter Seventeen	*Finding the Dreamer*	128
Chapter Eighteen	*The Agent*	135
Chapter Nineteen	*Transparent*	148
Chapter Twenty	*Mrs. Morice-Gilland*	156
Chapter Twenty-one	*The Creation*	165
Chapter Twenty-two	*Pralaya*	178
Chapter Twenty-three	*Breaking*	194
Chapter Twenty-four	*The Beginning of the End*	202
Chapter Twenty-five	*The Spark*	212
Chapter Twenty-six	*Word Magic*	221
Chapter Twenty-seven	*Flying*	232
Chapter Twenty-eight	*Shadows and Light*	235
Epilogue	*Another Ending, Another Beginning*	245

PROLOGUE
A Beginning

My name is Mehera Beatrice Crosby, I'm twelve years old, and I've never even been on an airplane. Five steps up a ladder and I freak out. I wouldn't go on a roller coaster if you paid me a gazillion dollars. So what the heck was I doing, scared half to death (and totally thrilled, too—in a stomach-turning kind of way), sailing over the North Carolina woods, riding a *winged lion* across the sky? I held tight—really, really tight—to Yalee's mane, trying with all my heart not to cry. But how could I not? I'd just watched a friend—a friend who, until recently, *had existed only in my imagination*—die. No, he didn't just die: He was murdered, right in front of me.

So much had happened, so fast, in just a few weeks, and now here I was, riding the back of a creature I'd only read about in books, chased by a living nightmare that wanted to destroy me. "Always follow your dreams," my mother used to tell me. "They may not lead you where you expect to go, but they'll always lead you someplace wonderful." Well, I'd followed my dreams and they'd led me someplace that didn't feel wonderful at all.

I turned to see if the nightmare was still behind us, and something hit me: It was like the sun exploded right in my face. The pain was awful. It didn't just burn my skin, it burned my mind. I actually think it might have burned my *soul*.

The mane slipped from my hands.

The lion roared.

I was falling.

CHAPTER ONE
Another Beginning

Three weeks before that—on a totally wretched, rainy April morning in Queenstown, New York (that's about a hundred miles north of New York City, in case you're interested)—I'd been standing in front of my seventh-grade English class, facing a different kind of danger. "The book I picked to talk about," I announced, "is the fourth book in the Imaginalis series: *Flight from Forever* by Mikela Morice-Gilland." I unrolled an old poster—it showed a boy with brown skin and gorgeous eyes flying on the back of a winged lion, while this elephant-headed creature with a fat Buddha belly was hanging on to the lion's tail for dear life—and tacked it into the corkboard.

There were groans from the back of the classroom. Sheryl Bernstein buried her face in her hands. Laura

Washington's hand shot up into the air. "Mrs. Young, Mrs. Young," she whined.

"What is it, Laura?"

"She did this already," Laura said, making sure Mrs. Young could tell how annoyed she was.

"Who did what?" Mrs. Young asked.

"*She* did," Laura said, pointing at me like she was picking out a serial killer in a police lineup. Look, I hate public speaking. I was so terrified before school that day, I nearly threw my guts up. Now, standing there all alone at the front of the classroom, I had to fight the urge to duck behind the teacher's desk or maybe run straight out the door. "*Mehera Crosby* did."

"I don't understand," Mrs. Young said.

"She's been doing it since the third grade. Any time there's a book report, it's the same stupid book over and over again." Laura turned to Sheryl. "Isn't that right? Isn't it?"

Sheryl lifted her head, rolled her eyes—"The same stupid book," she said—then buried her face in her hands again.

"It is *not* the same book, Mrs. Young," I said, keeping my eyes focused on the floor, the walls, anywhere but on *all those faces*. "There are four books in the Imaginalis series, and I remember for a fact that last year I did a report on the first one. And in fifth grade I did a report on the third one, and—"

"It's all right, Mehera," Mrs. Young told me. She turned to face the class. "The assignment," she said, in a tone that was really sweet but made it clear that she didn't want to hear another word from Laura or Sheryl, "was to pick your favorite novel. And that's just what Mehera did. Now everyone settle down and listen." That's why I adore Mrs. Young. She's the best teacher in the History of Teaching.

Laura gave me a nasty look, and I shot back with what I call the Famous Crosby Squint-Glare (that would be a combination of a totally withering squint and an absolutely devastating glare). In my mind, the squint-glare blasted Laura out of her seat, through the wall, and straight across Pearl Avenue into Johnny Dee's Pizzeria, but in reality, Laura shrugged, stuck out her tongue, and started doodling in her notebook.

"Now remember, Mehera," Mrs. Young added, "we don't want a summary of the entire book, just your favorite scene." I know that Mrs. Young really likes me—a couple of times a month she invites me to come to the teachers' cafeteria to have lunch with her, and we'll have an amazing time talking about books and movies and, well, anything but school—but she's still my teacher and she knows that my brain has a habit of racing in twenty zillion directions at once and when I start talking . . . well, it's kind of hard to keep me on track.

"Right. Okay." All of a sudden I felt so nauseatingly self-conscious, I thought I was going to faint. (I'm an expert fainter, too. Been doing it for years.) I fiddled with the buttons on my vest, tucked my hair—it's thick and frizzy and I'd pretty much hate it if it wasn't just like my mom's—behind my ears, then pushed it back into my face. I shuffled my notes, which I really didn't need. I knew *Flight from Forever* practically by heart. Then I looked over at Celeste Fishbein, who, after all, was my best friend (well, *Celeste* thought we were best friends—I wasn't so sure anymore). She flashed me this dopey grin that was so unbelievably fake—but, really, she was just trying to encourage me, and I've got to give her points for that.

"Okay," I finally said. "So." A deep breath. "My favorite scene comes at the very end of the book when Prince Imagos . . . he's the hero . . . when the series starts he's like seven, but by Book Four he's fifteen. Anyway, the Prince is in the Forever Forest"—there was snickering from the back of the class (Laura again)—"where he's found the Abrasax Mirror . . . which isn't really a mirror, it's this humongoid standing stone—y'know, like Stonehenge in

England?—but it's so polished it *reflects* like a mirror . . . and inside the Mirror is the image of the villain of the series, Pralaya. He can pretty much change into anyone or anything he wants, but now . . . and this is a really big moment in the series . . . now, for the first time, the Mirror is showing his *true form*. It's like his entire head starts to melt . . . and then the rest of him, too . . . till he's oozing and bubbling and he doesn't look *anything* like a human being anymore. He's just this big ball of gunk . . . slime just dripping off him . . . and he smells terrible, too . . . even through the Mirror . . . like the world's biggest toilet just overflowed. When he's in a human form, Pralaya's always using these supernatural perfumes to cover the scent . . . but not now. I mean, it's *totally* gross and Imagos is *totally* freaking out. It's all he can do not to barf right then and there."

More snickering. And not just from Laura this time. "Maybe dial back a little on the descriptions, Mehera," Mrs. Young said.

"Yeah, sure. Sorry." Me and my big dumb mouth. I stared straight down at the tips of my Doc Martens and refused to look up. "Anyway . . . all these eyes . . . ten, twenty, thirty eyes . . . just kind of appear in the surface of that gunk ball and they're all just *staring* at Prince Imagos. I mean, if looks could kill, Imagos would be dead a hundred times over. And then . . . *then* these octopus tentacles come shooting out . . . only they're *not* octopus tentacles, they've got the heads of *snakes* on the end . . . any one of them could kill you in a split second if they got their fangs into you. Just tear into your flesh, burrow their heads into your guts and—"

"Mehera?"

"Right. Sorry, Mrs. Y." Big. Dumb. Mouth. "So, anyway, all the gunk starts swirling around and then this mouth forms . . . right in the middle of this moun-tain of sewage . . . big fat lips . . . a grin like a totally wackazoid jack-o-lantern . . . and these teeth that're like elephant tusks. And the thing . . . the thing that used to be Pralaya . . . that *is* Pralaya, the *real* Pralaya . . . laughs. It says in the book that his laugh was like molten lava. Isn't that perfect? I mean, you can just hear it in your head, can't you? The sound of molten lava, if molten lava could laugh?" I looked up for a second, and it was pretty clear from the looks on the other kids' faces that they could all care less. The only ones who looked even vaguely inter-ested were Celeste and Andrew Suarez, who, for some stupid reason, had a mad crush on me. (The truth is, Andrew's totally girl crazy. He has crushes on *everyone*. I guess it was just my turn.) Laura, of course, was doing her best to look totally bored. Sheryl had her head down on her desk, like naptime in kindergarten. The rest of them were trying to pretend that they were interested— for Mrs. Young's sake, not mine—but they weren't very convincing. "Well, *I* could. Right away."

Eyes back on the shoes. Another deep breath. "Anyway, Pralaya, he starts talking to Imagos, in that molten-lava voice of his. 'Do you see now why you can't win, Prince?' Pralaya says. 'Do you see now why you can *never* win? I'm not even there with you. I'm half a world away, and you're ready to drop to your knees and surrender. You're no better than your pathetic father.'

"Well, when Imagos hears *that*, he can't help but remember what it was like when his dad, Rajah Merogji, was around . . . before Pralaya came back and murdered the Rajah and Imagos had to go into exile in the Forever Forest with this amazing group of characters called the Companions: there's Imagos's old tutor, Uncle Nossyss . . . the Prince's bodyguard, Shokra, and—"

"We don't need every detail, Mehera," Mrs. Young said gently. "Condense a little."

I wanted to condense *myself*. If it was up to me, I would have rushed through the rest of the scene, but Imaginalis was just too important. I had to go on. Not for me. *For the story*. "So Imagos is thinking about how it used to be and how much he misses his parents . . . his

9

mom, Queen Tara, died of a broken heart right after the Rajah was assassinated . . . and he's getting so mad he's not even thinking about the people of Imaginalis, he's just thinking about himself, about how much he wants to make Pralaya pay for what he's done.

"The Prince, he reaches into his quiver and pulls out one of the Eternity Arrows. They're these magical arrows that, if you use them right, they're the most powerful weapons in the world. But the problem is, Imagos has never even figured out how to really use them. *No one* has. But that doesn't stop him from trying again. He grabs the bow, pulls back the string . . . he's concentrating so hard, it's like he's putting all his anger, all his hatred, into the arrow . . . then Imagos lets the Eternity Arrow go . . . and wham! The Abrasax Mirror smashes into ten thousand tiny, glittery pieces that go swirling up into the air—and then there's just this burned-out stump left. And Pralaya is gone. But Imagos can still hear his voice, for just a second, hovering over the clearing. 'Fool,' the voice says. Just that one word: 'Fool.'

"Imagos realizes that destroying the Abrasax Mirror hasn't hurt Pralaya at all, and he just kind of drops to his knees . . . feeling like a total loser. And that's when this column of blue light sort of erupts out of the ground like a volcano. Not only that, but everything in the Forever

Forest goes dead quiet. No birds chirping, no wolves howling. Not even a breeze rustling a leaf. It's like time has stopped. Which it *has*. Imagos is stuck in time. 'He was trapped between the seconds.' That's the way Mrs. Morice-Gilland describes it in the book. Isn't that great?" I didn't have to look up to know that I was the only one who thought it was.

Another *really* deep breath. "Anyway, that's weird enough, but then Imagos notices that there's a *man* inside the light. And not just any man; it's his father. His *dead* father—Merogji, Rajah of the Swan, King of Dreamers, Lord of Believers. Rajah Merogji, he doesn't look dead at all . . . in fact, the guy looks better than he did when he was alive . . . and he steps out of the blue light and walks over to Prince Imagos. The Prince . . . he can't explain it, but he knows that this isn't some trick, *this really is his dad* . . . and he just wants to hug the Rajah, hold him, tell him how much he's missed him." That was when I *did* look up, just for a second, and noticed the way Zoe Traub and Simon Adams were both looking at me. And, I was sure of it, they were actually interested. Not in me, of course. *In the story.* I almost smiled, but decided that would break the spell. "And Imagos," I went on, "is telling Merogji how great this is, 'cause now they can work together to kill Pralaya and restore Imaginalis.

"But Merogji, he just pushes Imagos away. Not too hard or anything, but just enough to startle the Prince... and he tells his son that he can't embrace someone whose heart is filled with rage. Who's obsessed with revenge. 'Your years of exile have changed you,' the Rajah says. 'And not in ways that please me.' Imagos doesn't get it. He was just a little kid when his dad was killed ... and all this time he's been focused on one thing: getting the throne back, making Pralaya pay. And now his father's telling him that he shouldn't be doing that?

"The Rajah ... he does *not* sound happy ... tells the Prince that he's forgotten everything he learned when he was little. 'Compassion, not brutality,' Merogji says. 'That's the Imaginalian way. War and vengeance are things our people left behind centuries ago.' Imagos, he's starting to get a little angry. 'You wanna tell me how we can stop Pralaya *without* a little brutality?' And the Rajah, he says, 'Well, stopping him any other way would be completely impossible.' And Imagos is *really* confused now, 'cause it sounds like his father is *agreeing* with him. The Rajah smiles—this big grin like the Cheshire Cat—and he says, 'And that, my son, is the point.' Well, now Imagos is really *really* confused. 'Point?' he asks. "What point?'

"'Had we Imaginalians been locked in a prison of the

possible,' Merogji says, 'our kingdom would have collapsed eons ago.' Eons . . . that's like a *really* long time. 'It's only the impossible that has allowed us to survive.'

"Now listen to this," I said. It wasn't easy (in fact my hands started shaking and my legs went all wobbly), but I looked up then. Stared right out at all those faces. I had to. "I mean, *really listen.* 'Cause this is one of the best things I've ever heard. What he tells Prince Imagos is that most people . . . y'know, regular, boring people who live on regular, boring worlds like ours . . . they see the impossible as a . . ." It took me a few seconds to find the right word. "As a *limitation.* Something they can't have. 'Well, forget about that, right . . . why even try . . . it's impossible.' I mean, don't most of us say that all the time? But to an Imaginalian, the impossible is exactly what we should be reaching for. The unbelievable is exactly what we should believe in. It's like if you keep thinking that there are limits, you'll just keep doing things the same old way. But if you believe in the impossible . . . if you aim for it . . . and he uses that phrase a couple of times, 'aim for it' . . . then no matter what situation you're in, you'll always find a way out. You can change the whole world for the better. 'It's the impossible that brought Imaginalis into being—and that's what will bring it back.' Then Rajah Merogji gets this look in his eyes . . .

like he's going to cry or laugh, maybe both, Imagos can't tell . . . and he wraps his arms around his son, holds him so tight that the Prince feels like he's melting right into his dad, right through him. 'I love you, Imagos,' he says.

"And then, just like that, the Rajah of the Swan is gone. And time has started moving again. Imagos, he's crying now. He can't help it. He feels like he's lost his dad all over again. But he can't stand around feeling sorry for himself. He knows he has to rendezvous with the Borealis Boatman, journey across the Sea of Tears, and return home to Sheriar . . . that's the capital city of Imaginalis . . . 'cause that's where Pralaya is. He's got to go back there and restore the kingdom—but he sees now, thanks to his father, that he's got to do it in a new way. Without violence. Without even being angry. And how hard is that? Impossible, right? But that's what his father wants. He wants Imagos to do the impossible. At this point, he'd rather run back to camp, wake up the Companions, and beg them to come with him. But he has to go alone. According to Prognostica, the Nebulous Seer . . . she's this mystic type, very mysterious and a little weird and totally fun . . . the final showdown has to be between Pralaya and Imagos and nobody else.

"So the Prince grabs his pack and starts walking

down the Tenfold Trail . . . totally scared but, at the same time, braver than he's ever felt . . . when this voice booms down from the top of the trees. 'Hey,' the voice says, 'if you think you're going without me, then I'm gonna have to eat you.' Imagos turns around and there's Yalee . . . he's this mysterious winged lion who's not in the books all that much, but he always seems to show up when Imagos really needs him. Anyway, the Prince, he knows better than to argue with a lion, and besides, he's happy for the company. So he climbs up on Yalee's back. 'Let's go,' he says. 'Go where?' the lion asks. Yalee knows the answer, but he also knows that Imagos has to say it for himself. 'To the Port of Manija,' Imagos says . . . and the lion spreads his wings and they lift off into the air . . . sailing over the forest. 'To Manija—and the Sea of Tears.'

"And then comes the last line in the book. It's so simple and maybe it won't mean anything to you, but it gets me every time. 'And they flew off,' Mrs. Morice-Gilland writes, 'into the hope of night.'"

Andrew told me later that the bell rang just then and that some of the kids actually clapped and Mrs. Young had a big grin when she said, "Thank you, Mehera." But I didn't hear anything. I was so deep into Imaginalis that I couldn't see anything but Imagos and his winged lion, flying higher and higher, the sun setting in one direction, the moon rising in the other. "Do you get that?" I said. "I mean, usually it's the *dark* of night or the *dead* of night. People always talk about the night like that, right? Dangerous and creepy. But the *hope* of night? That really—"

"*Thank you*, Mehera," Mrs. Young repeated, and that time I heard her. I looked around, confused and disappointed, like I'd just been dragged, kicking and screaming, out of the most wonderful dream that had ever been dreamed. And that's the way it felt, too.

"Yeah, sure," I said, feeling like a first-class moron. I shoved my papers into my backpack, rolled up my poster, and ran out the door. I heard Celeste call out, "Hey, Mehera, wait up!"

But I disappeared faster than an Imaginalian sorcerer.

CHAPTER TWO
Celeste's Opinion

I didn't actually get a chance to talk to Celeste that afternoon, because I was on the bus and she was walking home—which was kind of nutty considering that we lived like four miles from the Queenstown Middle School. But Celeste, who had a habit of jumping from crazy fad to crazy fad, had been on a health kick lately. She'd stopped eating meat, had given up sugar, was only eating whole grains, and insisted on walking everywhere, even if the weather was horrible and she had to go ten miles. There was no way I was ever going to stop eating sugar or even touch tofu, but I figured that I could at least deal with walking home with her—at least until she got over her crazy health thing and moved on to something new. (As much as Celeste annoyed me, I didn't like the idea of her walking all that way alone.)

But I was feeling *totally* traumatized by my Imaginalis report, and I just wanted to get home as fast as I could. Plus, I knew Celeste. She was going to dissect the report like one of those disgusting frogs we peeled apart in biology. So I guess I was kinda sorta avoiding her.

The next day, Saturday, Celeste and her parents went to some kind of all-day folk music festival (sounds totally boring to me—I like Death Cab for Cutie and Leona Lewis and all that great old Beatles stuff my father's always playing), which was just fine with me, but I knew that, on Sunday, Avoiding Time would be over. You see, every Sunday morning since . . . well, since I can remember . . . I've gone to this place called Queenstown Family that sells old clothes and all kinds of other stuff to raise money for their food pantry. People who are having a hard time—maybe they've lost their job or they've been sick or they've just plain had bad luck and can't afford to buy food for their family—can come in and get whatever they need. And every Sunday morning there's this humongazoid breakfast—eggs and pancakes and waffles and bacon and cereal and bagels and you name it—and anyone can come in, pull up a chair and eat for free.

My mom—her name was Annie—was super involved with Queenstown Family. She ran fund-raisers and worked in the pantry a few afternoons a week (this was after she was done with her own work at the book-store my family owns), and every Sunday she'd be at the breakfast, cooking and serving and washing dishes and, most important, just being *nice* to the people who were there. "The smallest turn of fate, Mehera," she'd say, "and that could be us coming in here asking for help. These people aren't any different than we are. Only their circumstances are." Mama thought it was important that I come with her on Sundays and help. And I liked doing it. Still do.

Queenstown Family is where I first met Celeste. Her mother's an interfaith minister, and she was (and still is) even more involved with QF than my mom. She'd bring Celeste along with her Sundays, the same way my mom would bring me. There's this picture I love of both of us . . . I don't think we're even two years old . . . dishing out food—well, trying to, mostly we were just making a mess—while our moms hold us. After my mom passed away (you don't have to feel sorry for me, by the way. It was a long time ago and I'm okay. Really), I thought about not going to Queenstown Family anymore. In fact, I stopped for a month or two, but Reverend Fishbein con-vinced me to go back. She said it would make my mother happy. How could I say no to that?

That's why I knew I'd see Celeste that Sunday. I did

my best to stay out of her way most of the morning, but later on, we found ourselves washing dishes together. We'd been scrubbing away for maybe fifteen minutes, not really saying much—we could bounce text messages back forever, but talking face-to-face had been getting harder and harder lately—when Celeste finally said, "You did a great job with your book report."

"But?" I knew there was always a "but" where Celeste was concerned.

"Well, you could have picked another book. Don't get me wrong," she said, cutting me off before I could interrupt. "It's a terrific story and all . . . but, y'know, you really have done reports on Imaginalis like five hundred times before, and it's . . ." Celeste squinched up her face. "Y'know, for kids."

"We *are* kids," I said.

"We're not kids anymore," Celeste answered, looking all horrified and disgusted. "Pretty soon we'll be teenagers."

"Oh, really?" I answered. "Didn't you just finish reading *The Golden Compass* for like the third time? And isn't *that* a kid's book?"

"*The Golden Compass* is a *masterpiece*. The whole trilogy is. Pullman totally subverts the children's book genre to create an absolutely *devastating* critique of the absolute uselessness of religion."

"What'd you, memorize that out of a review?" I knew she was probably repeating something her father said. Celeste's dad is maybe the most opinionated person I've ever met. He can't read a book or watch a movie or even walk down the street without going off into some long, boring speech about it. He's also an atheist—which is weird, since Reverend Fishbein pretty much believes in *everything*. I just can't figure out how that works.

"Look, Mehera," Celeste said, "if you keep reading that stuff, people are gonna think you're a total nerd."

"First of all," I said, even though it was pretty obvious, "I'm never gonna stop reading it. Second of all," I went on, even though it was more obvious, "we *are* nerds."

Celeste had to admit that was sort of true. "But you know what my mom says? She says the kids who are nerds in middle school, who *seem* like nerds, anyway, they're the ones who grow up to be the smartest and usually the prettiest, too. The ones who go out there and change the world. All the kids who are so *popular* . . ." She said it like it was the worst word in the English language. ". . . and think they're so incredible when they're our age, most of them never amount to anything. They're just a bunch of idiots." Look, I may not have liked the popular kids, but I wouldn't call them idiots. Celeste, on the other hand, called *everyone* an idiot. It was her all-purpose insult. And anyway, even if Reverend Fishbein was right, what was so great about having an interesting life in another ten or fifteen years? I wanted one now.

We scrubbed plates and rubbed gunk out of pots and pans, not talking, for another ten minutes, until Celeste finally said the thing I knew she'd been wanting to say the whole time. "You know, you've *really* gotta get over this Imaginalis thing."

I tried the Famous Crosby Squint-Glare on her, but it failed miserably. Again.

CHAPTER THREE
An Ending

I was hating seventh grade. Totally hating it. Oh, my grades were okay and my teachers weren't total disasters—and Mrs. Young, of course, was the very best of the best—but the kids were all starting to get weird. The girls were all "Oh, he's so cute!" and the boys were all "Look! There's hair growing on my lip!" and really, aside from Celeste, I wasn't interested in hanging out with anyone. I used to have this group of girls—Lasarina Webster, Alana Sloane, Mia Clements, Aria Een, three or four others—who I hung out with all the time. We'd have sleepovers every weekend, eat pizza, watch movies, put on plays in the living room, run around the yard screaming and laughing like crazy people. But by seventh grade, it was pretty much just me and Celeste, the nerd twins. And it sometimes seemed like we were hanging out more out of habit then anything else. I mean, let's face it: If we dumped each other, what would we have left?

About the only thing that kept me going was knowing that the fifth book in the Imaginalis series, *The Sheriar Prophecy*, was coming out soon. At least it was supposed to. Problem was, it was supposed to come out the year after *Flight from Forever*—but that year came and went and so did the year after that, and . . . nothing. I checked the internet all the time, kept bugging my dad to find out anything he could (he had a friend who had a friend who had a friend who worked for Dreaming Press Children's Books, the company that published the Imaginalis series), but all he came up with was "It's coming, but not just yet." Not exactly helpful. All that waiting was driving me totally nutsoid. It was like waking up on Christmas morning, ready to tear open your presents, and finding out that the holiday had been postponed till the following December. "What," I asked Papa one night over bean burritos, "is *taking* so long?"

"You know," he answered, "a book isn't an easy thing to write. They don't just appear on the page like magic. Sometimes, well, the story's just not ready."

"Not ready?" I said, sighing. "*I* could have written the book by now. I could have written *five* books."

Papa smiled. "Well, then, why don't you?"

"Why don't I what?" I asked.

"Why don't you write the next book? You're a wonderful writer, Mehera Bea, and it would be fun, wouldn't it, to compare what you write with the actual book when it comes out?"

The truth was, I'd already written four or five of my own Imaginalis stories, these super-long epics starring . . . well, me. I know it sounds dopey and immature, and maybe it is, but I loved imagining myself as part of the story, helping Prince Imagos save the kingdom and then marrying him and, yes, maybe even kissing him at the end. I never showed those stories to anyone, never even admitted that they existed, and for a few seconds I was totally sure my father'd been poking around in my computer files and that my secret life had been exposed. Then I realized how dumb that was. My dad was a lot of things, but a snoop wasn't one of them. "Or maybe," he went on, "we could do it together."

A part of me thought that was just about the stupidest thing I'd ever heard—I mean, we hadn't made up stories together since I was *ten*—but another part of me thought it was pretty sweet. I almost said, "Sure, Papa, let's do that. Let's do it tonight." But the words that came out of my mouth, all obnoxious and sarcastic, were: "I'm not a little girl anymore, Papa." I got up, stomped over to the sink, scraped off my plate, and slid it into the dishwasher.

I looked over at Papa, and he had this look on his face like a puppy that'd been kicked down the stairs, and I was just about to apologize when he said, "Don't take that tone with me, Mehera Bea," in this megaserious voice he uses when he wants me to know that he's not just Papa—he's a parent, I'm his daughter, and I'd better listen to him or else. He really isn't very good at that voice—in fact, I don't think he likes using it. It's like he's acting, pretending to be someone he isn't.

"I'm not taking any tone," I said, even though I knew I was. I cleared the rest of the table—I didn't look at Papa and he didn't look at me—and then went up to my room to do my homework.

I grabbed my history book, gave it a seriously dirty look, and tossed it away. Then I picked up *Flight from Forever* and began reading it for the sixth time.

The next day, Celeste and I sloshed into A Thousand Voices. (That's the name of my dad's bookstore. It comes from an old Native American saying: "It takes a thousand voices to tell a single story.") It had started raining halfway home, and we were sopping wet. I could have called

Papa—I knew he would have dropped everything and picked us up—but the truth is, we were enjoying getting soaked. There was something so . . . I dunno . . . *free* about it. It made us feel like we were six years old again—putting on our bathing suits and playing mermaid in the big tub in my mom and dad's bathroom—back when we really *were* best friends. We giggled, we splashed each other. We filled our mouths with rainwater and then spit it in each other's faces.

The store was on the way home, and I always stopped by to check in with Papa. Even if I was taking the bus, I'd get off two stops early to see him: It made him feel better. And it made me feel better, too—especially after the dumb fight we'd had the night before. He was always happy to see us . . . except when we were dripping all over the merchandise.

"Wait, wait," Papa said as soon as he saw us. "Don't move a muscle." He raced into the back room, then came back with an a couple of towels. "Dry yourselves off. Leave your shoes on the mat."

A few minutes later, Celeste and I were sitting on stools, sipping hot orange spice tea and working our way through a kind of stale bag of Pepperidge Farm cookies. Celeste was flipping through a copy of *Les Misérables*. Her parents had taken her to see the Broadway play when she was ten and she'd loved it, but she'd tried to read the book three times and could never get more than a hundred pages into it before her brain started to melt. She was getting ready for a fourth try. Me, I was just staring into space, dipping my Milano into my tea and taking a bite, when, without really thinking, I turned to my father and asked the question I asked almost every day: "Any word about Imaginalis?" Papa, still wiping water off the floor, didn't hear me, so I asked him again.

When Papa turned around with this look of super-deluxe panic in his eyes, I knew something was wrong. "What?" I asked.

"Mehera—"

"What?"

"I found something out today. You're—you're not going to be happy about it."

"What?" I hopped off the stool and walked past the cookbooks and biographies.

Papa tried to say something, but nothing came out. He cleared his throat and tried again. "Imaginalis," he finally croaked.

"What about it?" I asked, my mouth clogged with milky, mashed cookie.

"I found out today . . . that is, my friend Denise, you know, the one who works at— Anyway, she heard from *her* friend over at—"

"Just tell me," I insisted.

"The fifth Imaginalis book . . . *The Sheriar Prophecy.*" He took a deep breath, then said, "It's not coming out."

"They delayed it *again?*" I couldn't believe it. "How long this time? Six months? Another year? This is ridiculous, Papa. When are they—"

"They didn't delay it, Mehera Bea."

"What?" I swallowed the rest of the Milano. "But you just said—"

"They *canceled* it."

"What do you mean, canceled?"

"It's not coming out, goose."

"What are you saying?" Actually, I knew exactly what he was saying, but I was hoping he was wrong. He *had* to be.

Papa got up. Put a hand on my head and stroked my hair. "The book *isn't coming out*," he said. "Not this year. Not ever. The Imaginalis series is over."

And that's when I fainted.

CHAPTER FOUR
Shock

"Mehera, get up," Papa said.

"Leave me alone, I'm unconscious," I answered.

"Up. Now." He sure didn't sound like a father who'd just watched his daughter collapse on the floor. In fact, he sounded pretty annoyed. Which I guess makes sense when you consider that I'd probably fainted like six thousand times before that, usually when I was excited or upset about something. Okay, so it wasn't *fainting* fainting. I didn't really black out or anything. It was more like the fainting I've seen in old movies. You know, where people put the backs of their hands to their foreheads, like they're posing for a picture, and kind of fall back in slow motion? But it's not like I was *pretending* to faint or anything because, really, when it was happening I totally believed it was the real deal. Well, almost. Okay, so I know that it's kind of weird and maybe immature, but I started doing it when I was little, maybe seven or eight . . . and I just couldn't stop. Papa was really scared at first, and he took me to a whole bunch of doctors, but none of them seemed very worried about it. They said it was a phase and that I'd get over it—and I guess I did. I mean, when I was younger, I used to faint all the time—maybe once a week—but by the seventh grade I only did it once in a while. When it was important. And the end of the Imaginalis series was about as important as it got.

"Get up," Papa repeated, reaching down, taking my hand, and helping me to my feet. "Really, Mehera Bea, you're getting too old for this."

"Too old for what?" I said, as annoyed as he was. "You think I'm faking? I'm in *shock*, in case you haven't noticed. I'm *devastated*."

"Look, sweetie," Papa said, "I know you're upset about this, I know how much the Imaginalis books mean to you, but—"

"You can't possibly know!" I squealed. I put a hand against my forehead and almost fainted again, but Papa gave me one of those looks and stopped me cold. I turned to Celeste, who'd been watching us like we were some kind of TV reality show. "C'mon," I said, "let's go."

Papa gave me a quick peck on the top of my head. "It'll be okay, goose," he said.

"Easy for you to say. My entire world has been destroyed."

Papa ignored that. "When you get home," he said, "don't forget to cut up the veggies for tonight's stir-fry."

"I can't think about food," I said, staggering out the door like I was carrying a mountain on my back. "I don't think I'll ever eat again."

I don't think Papa was very worried about me starving—and, honestly, neither was I—because he knew that I usually eat twice as much when I'm upset. I'm on the skinny side, like my mom. Dad says she was one of those people who could eat whatever she wanted and never gain a pound, and I'm pretty much the same way. In fact, that night, after I stuffed my face at dinner, I was up in my bedroom doing my homework and pigging out on a bowl of pretzels, raisins, and dry cereal—my favorite snack in the world.

Usually when my homework's done, I go into what I call the Zone-Out Zone, texting Celeste or maybe wasting an hour or two on Facebook and MySpace and all those goofy sites. I've got like a million friends online. They're not *friend* friends. On the internet you pretty much talk to any kid, even the ones you wouldn't even *look* at if you passed them in the hall. My dad doesn't get that, and I can kind of see why it confuses him. I guess the truth is that when I'm talking to people online, not having to deal with them face-to-face, I can relax in a way I can't at school. I don't feel clumsy or shy, weird or funny looking, I just feel like . . . Mehera. It works the other way around, too: Kids are a lot less annoying when they're just a block of text on a screen.

But that night I wasn't on the computer. I was sitting on my bed, looking up at the Imaginalis poster—the same one I'd taken to school for my report—on the wall above my bed. I may have said it in a big, dramatic way, but I meant it when I told Papa that my world had been destroyed. Imaginalis, *my Imaginalis*, was gone, and it was never coming back. I sat there wondering how I could go on living without *The Sheriar Prophecy* to look forward to. And I wasn't just worried about how *I* would go on, I was worried about the *characters*, too. I wondered what would happen to Prince Imagos and Uncle Nossyss, Pralaya, Prognostica, and all the rest without me reading about them? Where would they go? Would they even exist anymore?

Okay, so that sounds totally crazy—but, take my word for it, it wasn't *half* as crazy as it seemed at the time.

CHAPTER FIVE
Dear Mrs. Morice-Gilland

Over the next couple of weeks, I wrote a bunch of letters (well, maybe more than a bunch. Maybe a few dozen) to this woman Dawn Berger, the Imaginalis editor at Dreaming Press Children's Books. At first I didn't hear anything back, but then I actually got a phone call from Miss Berger. She was totally sweet and we talked for almost half an hour, but she also made it pretty clear that the Imaginalis books were over and there was nothing she could do about it. That's when I figured, hey, what does an editor know? So I started writing to the company's president, vice president, proofreader, receptionist, security guard, cleaning person, anyone at Dreaming Press who might be able to do something to bring the series back again. When my dad got an email from that friend of a friend of a

friend telling him to tell me to stop—and she wasn't
nice about it, either—I swore I wouldn't write any more
letters. And I didn't.

That's when I started the Bring Back Imaginalis
petition, but I couldn't even convince Celeste to sign it.
(You know what she told me? "Get over it." Nice, huh?) I
thought about forging a few thousand names, but I'm not
very good at being dishonest. (I know this girl at school,
Harriet Chalk, and she can lie about *anything* without
it ever bothering her. In fact, she seems to enjoy it. I
just don't get that. I'm the kind of person who gets all
totally guilty if I so much as look at someone else's test
answers by accident.) I went to the message boards at the
Imaginalis website to see if I could find any other fans to
help me, but the boards had been taken down. (A week
later, the whole site was gone.)

I was getting seriously depressed. And seriously
worried.

One afternoon, I was having lunch with Mrs.
Young—I think I told you that she lets me do that sometimes, we eat our sandwiches and talk about all kinds of
stuff—and she suggested that I write directly to Mikela
Morice-Gilland and tell her how much her Imaginalis
series meant to me. "I'm sure she'd be totally delighted
to hear from you, Mehera," Mrs. Young said. I thought

that was an amazing idea and spent almost a week writing the letter.

Dear Mrs. Morice-Gilland,

The first thing you should know is that my father owns a bookstore and that we sell all your Imaginalis books. In fact, I made a special display—well, my friend Celeste helped me—for the series, and it says right on it, "Best! Books! Ever!" The downstairs of our store is for all the bestsellers and ancient stuff like Oliver Twist and Catcher in the Rye and travel books and all the stuff you'd expect, and the upstairs is for children's books. That's where the Imaginalis display is, just a couple of feet from this great big banner that hangs over the archway when you walk in: Life itself, *the banner says,* is the most wonderful fairy tale—Hans Christian Andersen.

I guess growing up around books, and around Papa, is what made me into such a first-class "story beast." (That's what he calls me.) Papa says that from the time I was little, I was hungry for stories. Totally desperate for them. When other kids were reading books about ABCs and fuzzy puppies, I was asking for chapter books, the longer the better. Papa used to read to me almost every night before bedtime.

and I'm okay. Really.) Papa had to go to this gigantor book fair in New York City and I was supposed to stay with my friend Celeste's family while he was gone, but neither of us really wanted to be apart (I guess you can understand why), so he took me along. Well, the whole thing was unbelievably boring—just a lot of grown-ups talking and talking and talking—and I probably drove him crazy with my whining, but the one really amazing part was that the publishers were giving away free copies of their new books. Free! We filled four canvas bags with goodies, mailed those to the store, then filled six more. It wasn't until we got home that I came across this super-fat hardcover written and illustrated by an author named (ta-daaaaa!) Mikela Morice-Gilland. I remember looking at the cover of The Prince of Imaginalis and trying to figure out what was going on. Okay, so there was a boy who was close to my own age—he looked like he'd stepped out of an Arabian Nights story—being carried along a dark hallway by this humongously fat creature that seemed to be half human and half elephant. Next to the elephant guy was this woman who looked like Rapunzel, only with her hair on backward, covering the whole front of her body (and maybe the back, too—you couldn't really tell from the picture).

The three of them were being chased by . . . well, it was hard to tell what was chasing them. Just eyes, mostly. Twenty or so totally creepy eyes that scared the heck out of me (don't forget, I was just a little kid then). But I think, in a weird way, those eyes are what made me want to read the book. (Okay, I know you know what was on the cover—I mean, you painted it yourself—but I want you to understand what it was like for me, seeing it for the first time.)

I told Papa that we had to read The Prince of Imaginalis that night, and from the first words— "You may think this is just a fairy tale, but I swear to you it's the truth"—I was hooked. It was like I'd been waiting my whole life to hear that story. Like some part of me had known that world, and every character in it, for years and years, and now I was meeting them all again for the first time. (I know that sounds kind of crazy. Or maybe not. I figure since you created Imaginalis you must feel the same way. At least I hope you do.) I wasn't just listening to my father reading about Imaginalis, I was living in it. It really felt like the book had been written and published just for me. As soon as we finished it, I had Papa read it to me again. And again. And then I read it myself, three or four times.

It didn't take me long to decide that you were the Greatest Writer in the History of Writing, better than Shakespeare and Dickens and J. K. Rowling put together (and I'm not just saying that, I really truly mean it) and I wanted to know everything there was to know about you. All the book jacket had to say was that you were born in England but spent your childhood in India, then got married and moved to the United States. Well, that wasn't nearly enough information for me (although I was thrilled that you used to live in India, because my parents went there a long time ago, before I was born, and I bet you don't want to hear about that, either, do you?), and I looked on the internet for more. Unfortunately, there wasn't any. That upset me at first, but I figured I'd find out all about you when we met. You see, I knew, from the time I finished The Prince of Imaginalis, *that we were going to meet one day and that the two of us would become the very best of friends and discuss all the secret things we thought and felt but would never share with anyone else (okay, so I didn't really have any secret things to share. But I figured I could come up with something before we finally met).*

I kept reading your books, year after year, and I swear each one was better than the one before and I just loved the series more and more. No, I didn't just love it: I believed it. Although I never actually said it out loud to anyone—truth is, I was even embarrassed to admit it to myself—I was kinda sorta convinced I wasn't from Earth at all. I was an Imaginalian, sent here by a dark wizard (maybe Pralaya himself—by the way, he has got to be the coolest, creepiest villain ever) and trapped in the body of a skinny twelve-year-old girl with a pimple smack in the middle of her nose that keeps coming back no matter what I do about it. Anyway . . .

The point is, I love Imaginalis more than I've ever loved any book in the History of Reading. Prince Imagos and Uncle Nossyss and all your characters have become my Closest Absolute Very Best Friends. (I know that must sound weird, but since you're the one who created them, maybe it doesn't.) Imaginalis is my home. It's the place I most want to be. The place I always go back to.

And that's why, Mrs. Morice-Gilland, you just have to have to HAVE TO write the next book and get it published, even if you just put the whole thing on the internet yourself. (I bet you'd get like a gajillion downloads, too.) If The Sheriar Prophecy doesn't come out, and soon, I don't know what I'm

going to do—aside from being super-deluxe depressed
for the rest of my life—but I'm not going to worry
because I know you won't let me down.

Your Biggest Fan,

Mehera Beatrice Crosby

I sent the letter to Dawn Berger. She didn't bother to answer, but her assistant wrote to tell me they would forward it to Mrs. Morice-Gilland's agent, Gerald Epstein. Well, that was pretty exciting, until Mr. Epstein wrote back to me to say that "My client guards her privacy fiercely and never reads letters from her readers under any circumstances."

When I told Celeste what had happened, this is what she said: "Life can really suck sometimes." For once, I agreed with her. I mean, I'd tried everything. There was no one left to ask for help. And then I had either the best, or maybe the stupidest (or maybe both), idea in the History of Ideas.

Why not ask the Imaginalians themselves?

CHAPTER SIX
Come Back

I stood on my bed, in front of the Imaginalis poster, running my hand over those faces that I loved so much. "I know this is crazy," I said. "Maybe I'm totally losing it . . . but I believe in you . . . I swear I do . . . I believe in you more than I believe in"—I looked out the window at the houses and the night sky, and all of a sudden everything looked as fake as the painted backdrops they used for the cheesy musicals they put on at my school—"any of this. And you can't go away, you just can't." I swear, for a second it seemed like Uncle Nossyss's eyes twinkled and he winked at me. "You *have* to come back. I can't live without you. *You have to come back.*" I felt tears running down my face; I'd been crying the whole time and hadn't even realized it. "You have to—"

"Mehera?" At first I thought it was Uncle Nossyss answering me (dumb, huh?), but it was only my dad, who was down the hall doing laundry.

"What?" I called back, annoyed at the interruption.

"You on the phone? I told you, no calling, no texting after ten. You—"

"I'm not on the phone."

Papa showed up in the doorway, looking as annoyed as I was. "But I heard you—" When he saw the tears, his annoyance just kind of melted away. "Honey, what is it? What's wrong?" he asked. Papa tries hard sometimes to seem like he's the big tough parent, but I know that if I get so much as a scrape on my knee, he freaks. One tear, and he melts into a puddle. Which is why, as soon as he saw how upset I was, he sat down on the bed and put his arms around me.

"It's stupid," I said. I was crying so much now I could hardly get the words out. "It's nothing."

"Tell me, sweetie."

I pushed my face up against his chest and said: "I miss them, Papa."

"Miss who, goose?"

"My *friends*."

"You mean Alana and Aria and the whole gang you and Celeste used to—"

"No," I said, cutting him off, annoyed again. How could he even *think* I meant them? "I'm talking about Prince Imagos and Uncle Nossyss and the Imaginalians."

"The . . . Imaginalians?" I thought he was going to get annoyed at me when I said that—and maybe he was—but something, maybe the pathetic look on my face, stopped him. "I understand," he said. "I really do. I remember when I was about fifteen and I read *Lord of the Rings* for the first time. It swept me away, right out of Brooklyn. Right out of this world. God, I loved those books. I loved those characters. And when I got to the end . . . it hurt. It actually hurt. And remember," he went on, nuzzling his chin against the top of my head (he needed a shave and it was kind of scratchy. But *good* scratchy), "remember when you were . . . what? Six? The first time we read the Narnia books? We got to the last page of the last book and both of us were so sad it was over that we could hardly talk."

"It's not the same," I whispered.

"Not exactly the same, but you—"

"You don't *understand*," I said, scooting away from him just a little. "Those books were over. They were finished. The stories were complete. But this one . . . this one *isn't* over. There were supposed to be three more books. The Imaginalians are stuck, Papa. It's just like what happened in *Escape to Nolandia.*"

"Remind me," Papa said.

I couldn't help myself: I rolled my eyes. I mean, how could someone read a book as amazing as *Escape to Nolandia* and then forget what happened? "Prince Imagos and the Companions are on the run, and they find a doorway into Nolandia . . . that's this weird limbo place where everything is . . . well, it's all nothing. A humongous, endless ocean of nothing, and if you stay there too long, you can't *ever* get out. Eventually everyone you've ever known forgets about you and you just turn into a shadow . . . then the *shadow* of a shadow . . . and then—"

"Mehera. I'm sorry, sweetie, but what's the point?"

I rolled my eyes again. "The point is it feels like that's where they are now. *Stuck in limbo.* And if I don't do something, then one day they're all just going to turn into shadows and fade away and no one's going to remember them. Not even me."

Papa ran a hand through his hair—well, what was left of it. He was pretty bald. "I don't think you'll ever forget them, goose," he said.

"But," I answered, really scared, "what if I do?"

Papa thought that over for almost a minute. "Mehera," he finally said, "you know I believe that there's nothing more wonderful than a great book. That's why I have the store, because I want kids, I want everyone, to understand that . . . to feel it the way you do. But still . . ." I could tell he wasn't sure if he should say it, but he did, anyway. "It's just a book, goose. It isn't real. It—"

"It *is* real!" I know I shouldn't have yelled like that, but he made me so angry. "More real than . . ." I was so upset I could hardly get the words out. "Than you!"

"You mean I'm not real?" He started poking at himself. "I certainly *feel* real enough." He was trying to get me to laugh, but I didn't think it was funny. In the least.

"*You don't understand,*" I said again. "Nobody does."

"Mehera, honey, I've been hiding behind mountains of books my whole life. There's *nobody in the world* who understands better than I do."

I pushed myself back against the wall, folded my arms across my chest, and turned away from him. "God, I hate my stupid life."

Papa's voice got really quiet then. "Is your life really that bad?" he said—and he sounded kind of sad.

I turned back to face him. "It's not you, Papa. I know you do your best. I *know* you do. You can't help it if you're—"

"If I'm what, goose?"

"If you're not an Imaginalian. If you don't . . . if you

don't *believe* enough. Merogji said—"

"Who?"

I rolled my eyes *again* and threw in a big groan, too, just to make sure he noticed. I mean, didn't he remember *anything* about the books? "The Rajah of the Swan. Imagos's father. He said that if we believe in the impossible . . . *really believe* . . . we can change the entire world."

"And do you," Papa asked, "believe enough?"

"Yes. No. Oh, I don't know. I guess I'd like to."

"Well, then, maybe you will. Change the world."

I turned away again. "Or leave it," I mumbled.

"What?"

"Leave here . . . and go to Imaginalis. That's where I'd like to live. That's where I belong."

"Don't say that, goose. Don't ever say that."

"What?"

"Don't you *ever* talk about leaving me."

"But I'm just—"

My father may get annoyed at me sometimes, but he doesn't get angry very often, and he almost never raises his voice. That night he did both. "You're almost thirteen years old, Mehera. *Thirteen.* Time to get your head out of the clouds." He stood up on the bed and started to peel the Imaginalis poster off the wall.

"Papa!"

"Time to grow up!"

"Papa, no!"

I jumped to my feet, grabbed onto the poster, trying to yank it away from him, and Papa grabbed back, the two of us bouncing and rocking on the mattress like it was a trampoline. It took about three seconds for the poster to rip, part of it in Papa's hands, the rest in mine. I looked down, totally horrified, then up at him.

"I hate you!" I screamed. (I didn't hate him, not even when I said it, but it just came out and I was so mad there was no way I was going to take it back.)

I could tell that Papa felt bad. That a part of him wanted to apologize, but he wasn't going to take it back, either. He hopped off the bed. "Go to sleep," he growled. "It's almost eleven and you've got school tomorrow." He looked at the torn poster-half in his hand—with this kind of sick expression on his face—and then put it down on my desk.

"I hate you!" I screamed again. It was bad enough when I said it the first time. Don't ask me why I had to go and repeat it.

Papa turned and looked at me—I could tell he really wanted to say something but he couldn't find the right words—then left.

I sat on the bed staring at the door, then walked over to the desk and grabbed the other half of the poster. "Come back," I said, taping the two pieces back together. "Come back," I said again. I slipped under the covers, turned out the light, holding tight to the poster the way I used to hold on to my favorite furry blanket when I was a little kid. (I slept with that thing every night till I was nine.) Even though I was upset—or maybe because of it—I started to fall asleep pretty quickly . . . and, while I was drifting off, I could hear those words repeating in my head, over and over:

"*Come back . . . come back . . . come back. . . .*"

CHAPTER SEVEN

Contact

The next morning I woke up to the sound of my cell phone vibrating with a new text message. It was three words, all caps: HELP US, MEHERA! I didn't recognize the sender's name: UNSYS. I checked my contact list to see who it was, but when I looked up UNSYS, it wasn't in there. Which was impossible. If someone's not in my contact list, the display only shows a phone number. If a screen name shows up, it's because I added it myself. Which meant that UNSYS *had* to be on the list. But she—or he—wasn't. So how did UNSYS get in there and what did that message mean? HELP US, MEHERA!

I should have been brushing my teeth, picking out my clothes, rushing downstairs to grab breakfast, but instead I sat on the floor and typed back: WHO ARE YOU? A minute later my phone vibrated and the same message reappeared: HELP US, MEHERA!

This had to be one of the kids from school I texted with, goofing around with me. The first person I thought of was Alana Sloane, who was so immature that she still thought it was funny to order pizza and send it to someone else's house. We'd been super close all through grade school, but now we hardly looked at each other. ALANA, IS THAT YOU? I replied.

There was another vibration and then the same message: HELP US, MEHERA!

"Mehera!" Papa called from downstairs. "Hurry up, honey, or you're gonna be late. And if you're late—"

"Then *you're* late, too," I answered. We had the same conversation every morning, Papa hurrying me along, threatening to stop driving me to school and make me take the bus if I was late *one more day*—even though we both knew that, no matter how late I was, he'd always drive me.

The school bus takes forever to get to the middle school, so having Papa drive means that I have an extra half hour in the morning. Time to get my makeup right (it's just the tiniest bit of eyeliner, a smear of lip gloss, and some cover-up for my zits, so tell me why it seems to take longer every day). Time to pick out my clothes (not exactly a major decision, since I pretty much wear the same thing every day: an old vest of Papa's over a white blouse that's tucked into one of the Gypsy-type skirts I scavenged from my mom's closet. All finished off by a pair of Doc Martens that I'd worn practically to pieces). Time to actually eat some breakfast before we run out the door (although Papa usually cooks up a couple of scrambled eggs and some toast and I end up gobbling it down in the car). Some mornings we'd pick up Celeste, who only lives a few blocks away—but since she was on her walking kick it was just the two of us, and really, I kind of liked it better that way. It's not that Papa and I spent our time alone discussing Big Important Things. It was more like we'd just sort of hang out and *be* with each other . . . if you know what I mean . . . and there was something really sweet about that. That morning, neither one of us said a word about what had happened the night before, but we joked a little bit and talked about what we were going to have for dinner later, and I knew we'd pretty much apologized already, without really saying it.

Papa had one rule in the car: no cell phones. If he was going to drive me to school, he wanted us to be together, he didn't want me text-messaging half the galaxy. But that morning I couldn't help herself. While Papa wasn't looking, I turned the phone on and, sure enough, there were six new messages, two from Celeste and four from

down the contact list. "It's gotta be in here somewhere," she said. I snatched the phone back and shot Celeste the squint-glare, which—of course—failed again.

"I'm telling you, it's Andrew," Celeste said. "He's totally hot for you. And the guy knows everything about computers and cell phones and *all* that techno stuff. If anyone could slip some fake screen name past you, it's Andrew Suarez."

"But how do we prove it?"

Celeste's eyes lit up. "Why don't you," she asked, excited, "text this UNSYS right now?" She pointed across the cafeteria. "Andrew's right over there. If it's him, he'll pick up his phone and we'll know."

"Hey," I said, pretty impressed, "you're almost as good as Nancy Drew."

"*Nancy Drew?*" Celeste said, sounding like her father again. "I can*not* believe you still read that. I mean, it's formulaic garbage. Same recycled story in every book, they just change the stupid names around."

I wanted to pour my juice over Celeste's head, but instead I looked across the room. Sure enough, there was Andrew Suarez, five tables over, sitting with Herb Fillmore, both of them laughing at some stupid, crude boy joke. Most of the boys had somehow managed to get dumber, more obnoxious, and really, really foulmouthed since the beginning of seventh grade. My dad says it's all hormones and that they'll settle down in a few years. Why don't I believe that? "Okay, Andrew," I said. "Game's over."

The two of us turned, watching every move Andrew made, as I typed I KNOW WHO YOU ARE, UNSYS, then hit Send. I did it under the table, making sure none of the Dreaded Cafeteria Ladies (who'd confiscate your phone in a second; I think it actually makes them happy to do it) saw. I waited, totally sure now that it was him and so totally mad because he'd somehow gotten hold of my phone and messed around with it.

Andrew kept laughing and shoveling french fries into his big mouth. If his phone rang or buzzed, he didn't show it. "Maybe the idiot knows you're watching him," Celeste said. "Or maybe he's afraid that if he takes his phone out, the Cafeteria Ladies'll get it."

"Give it another minute," I answered. "He's definitely gonna—" My phone suddenly vibrated in my hand. Another incoming message. From UNSYS.

"That's spooky," Celeste said.

"Maybe it's *not* Andrew," I said.

"Or maybe," she suggested, "he's got one of his idiot friends doing it, just to throw you off the track." She slid up close to me, grabbed the phone again. "What's it say?"

I snatched it back. "Hands off, okay?" I snapped.

"Geez, I'm just kidding around," Celeste said. "What're you getting so mad about?" Celeste thought "just kidding around" was the perfect excuse for everything.

I stared at the message. It was different this time: STAND BY, the message said. And, then, one more word: BELIEVE. "Believe in *what*?" Celeste asked, leaning over my shoulder. I didn't think about the answer, it just sort of came out, all on its own: "The unbelievable," I said. I wasn't sure why, but I had chills. The hair on my arms was standing up.

CHAPTER EIGHT
The Cocoon

No more messages from UNSYS showed up that day, and weird as it sounds, I was kind of disappointed. I don't know, maybe I secretly hoped that Andrew really *had* sent them and that I *was* this week's Love of His Life. (Let me get this straight: I had zero interest in being Andrew's girlfriend, but I had to finally admit—to myself, at least—that it was nice thinking someone, even someone like Andrew, could feel that way about me, if only for a couple of days.) But the more I thought about it, the more I was sure that it *wasn't* Andrew sending the messages and that my disappointment came from . . . well, I couldn't really say. But it was there, anyway—and not just disappointment. It was like—and I know this sounds weird, too—I was looking for answers to questions I couldn't even think of.

"Where's your head tonight?" Papa asked over dinner.

I poked at my baked chicken, jammed a fork in my Japanese yam, then bit the end off a green bean. For a second I thought maybe I'd tell him about UNSYS the Mysterious, but then I changed my mind: Papa being Papa, I figured, he'd turn into a major nervous wreck about it, and the next thing you know, he'd be calling Reverend Fishbein or my teachers or maybe even the Queenstown police, demanding that UNSYS be tracked down and locked up in jail. "Nothing," I answered. Then I kind of snuck my phone out of my vest pocket, slipped it under the table—hoping Papa wouldn't see— and checked for messages. There were four, but none from UNSYS.

"Put the phone away," Papa said.

"If you're ever looking for a new career," I answered, "you oughta consider being a Cafeteria Lady."

That night there was another message, but this time it was on my Facebook wall, which, with all the privacy restrictions Papa makes me put up, should have been impossible. But there it was. "IMAGINALIS IS IN TROUBLE AND YOU'RE OUR ONLY HOPE," the message said. But it wasn't signed UNSYS this time, it was signed UNCLE NOSSYSS. I had to reread it a couple of times—Imaginalis? Uncle Nossyss?—before I came to the sickening conclusion that this wasn't some great mystery, this was just one of those idiots at school pulling a lame joke. And this was one time I wouldn't have argued with Celeste; they *were* idiots for going out of their way to make fun of the one thing they all knew I loved so much. I stared at the name on the screen for a while, then, suddenly figuring it out, let out a major groan. Grabbing a sheet of paper out of my printer, I wrote

UNCLE NOSSYSS

in the center of the page, then scratched out the middle block of letters and the S on the end until it looked like this:

UN~~CLE NO~~SSYS~~S~~

"Great," I mumbled, so mad I almost punched the wall. (I would have, too, except I actually did it once when I was around nine and hurt my hand so bad you can bet I'll never try that again.) How, I wondered, could I have been *so dumb?* How could I have let this creep trick me? "Whoever you are," I typed, "why don't you go bother someone else, because I don't think you're funny in the least. I think you're incredibly immature and incredibly dumb and if you do it again, I'm reporting this to the FBI." (Papa would have really liked that last part.) I hit the reply button, but, when I did, my computer instantly crashed. I rebooted it, went back to Facebook, tried resending the reply—but the computer crashed again. For an instant I was totally sure that this UNSYS person was somehow *stopping* me from replying, but that would have been impossible, too.

For the next two days I didn't hear a peep from UNSYS or Uncle Nossyss or whoever it really was. At school, I started checking everyone out, looking for likely suspects. (The truth is, I really do love Nancy Drew—I don't care if certain people think I'm getting too old for it—and I've always wanted to be a master detective.) First I was totally sure it *was* Andrew, then I just knew it was Alana, then I *absolutely* knew that it was, that it *had* to be, Laura Washington. Until I woke up at two in the morning, suddenly realizing that it wasn't Laura at all. *It was Celeste.* I mean, it made perfect sense. Wasn't Celeste the one who had told me to get over "this Imaginalis thing"? And wouldn't it be just like Celeste—anyway, it seemed that way in the middle of the night—to do something so incredibly hurtful and mean? I decided right then and there that my friendship with Celeste was finally over. We didn't really have anything in common anymore, anyway. We'd just been *pretending* to be friends for months, maybe years. Maybe always.

The next day I stopped talking to Celeste in school, stopped walking home with her, told Papa that he was *never* to give Celeste a ride in the morning *ever again*. (When he asked why, I just folded my arms across my chest and gave him the squint-glare. It was totally useless, of course.) I wouldn't even answer Celeste's texts, and that's pretty much the worst insult ever. But it wasn't just Celeste. THE UNSYS INCIDENT—that's the way I saw it in my head, in BIG BOLD LETTERS—had pretty much turned me off to everyone at school, except for Mrs. Young. And the way I was feeling, I didn't even want to talk to her. I decided that I was going to become a caterpillar and grow a cocoon around myself, one that *no one* was *ever* going to get through. And none of this sprouting wings and becoming a butterfly, either.

I was staying a caterpillar forever.

CHAPTER NINE
The Elephant

The morning of the third day—it was a Saturday and I was in my room, surfing the web and kinda sorta sulking—I received an instant message. "User Nossyss would like to send you an instant message. Will you accept?"

"Fat chance, Celeste," I said, then hit Don't Accept.

The message came through anyway.

"Mehera," the IM said, "it!s not Celeste, it!s not Laura, it!s not Andrew, it!s REALLY me. It!s Uncle Nossyss."

"Leave me alone," I typed back.

"I can!t leave you alone. You!re our only hope. Imaginalis will perish without you."

There was something in that last sentence that stopped me cold. For a second—I couldn't say why—it felt like the whole world got kind of shaky, like everything could just split apart, right in front of my eyes. Then the second passed. "Good one, Celeste," I said. "Bug off, you obnoxious twit," I typed.

"We!re trapped, Mehera" came the reply. "Only the Bridge can save us."

I typed back— "Leave! Me! Alone!"—then shut the computer down. I was so upset, I didn't even feel like reading. Just went out on the back porch and rocked in the hammock for hours, staring at the ceiling and thinking of all the Truly Awful Things I could do to get back at Celeste. I knew I'd never actually *do* any of them, but (and I know this sounds terrible) it was kind of fun to imagine, anyway. Then I started thinking about my mom and Reverend Fishbein and what good friends they'd been and how the fact that Celeste and I were such good friends, too, made them both so happy, and I started to feel kind of guilty about all those Truly Awful Things I'd been thinking. I wondered what Mama would say, and I was pretty sure that she'd tell me how important friendship is and how we should forgive each other because nobody's perfect. Except I didn't know *how* to forgive Celeste, and maybe I didn't want to. And that just made me feel worse.

That night when I turned on the computer again, there was an email waiting for me—which was weird, since most kids my age don't even bother with email, they're always texting, IMing, and Facebooking. In fact, most of the emails I get are from my father—he's always sending me articles he reads online or some video clip he thinks I'll enjoy. But this wasn't from Papa, it was from nossyss@saveimaginalis.com. "SaveImaginalis dot com?" I said out loud—and I swear it was like someone blasted me right between the eyes with a lightning bolt. All of a sudden, I wondered if this whole thing—the texts, the Facebook messages, the IMs—didn't have anything to do with Celeste at all. Maybe, I thought, it's some kind of publicity campaign to bring the Imaginalis series back. Maybe the publisher actually listened to me and they set up some new website and—

I didn't even bother to read the email, just typed www.saveimaginalis.com into the browser. A few seconds later, a message came up: "Sorry. We couldn't find saveimaginalis.com."

"Okay," I said, "so maybe they haven't set up the new site yet. Maybe they're just trying to get people interested. Well," I went on, opening the email, "it's working."

The email was short: "Follow this link," it said. And beneath that:

http://www.youtube.com/watch?v=izIpU9WxNOSYSS

I clicked and waited for the video to load. The more I thought about it, the more I was sure that Imaginalis was coming back and this YouTube video was just the beginning. Mrs. Morice-Gilland must have turned in her manuscript after all—maybe my letter had inspired her—and Dreaming Press Children's Books must have realized how incredibly stupid they were to cancel the series and it was *really happening*. I'd believed in the impossible, and now my dreams were coming true.

The YouTube page came up, and there, in black letters at the top of the screen, were the words A Message for Mehera from Uncle Nossyss. At first that confused me . . . maybe even scared me a little . . . but then I realized that it was pretty easy to do things like that with computers. Once I'd typed my name into a Disney site and, in a couple of seconds, I watched a Disney World video that had my name showing up on signs and rides all over the park. I figured if they could do that, they could sure do this.

I hit Play.

The screen was dark for a few seconds, and then Uncle Nossyss appeared. I almost fell out of my chair when I saw him. I mean, I knew it had to be a computer-generated image, but he looked *so incredibly real*. With his huge belly hanging over his belt and his trunk all coiled up on his lap like a snake, Nossyss looked even more real than he did in Mrs. Morice-Gilland's illustrations. There was this medallion thingy (in the books it's called an amulet and it has all kinds of mystical power) spinning around on his chest like a tiny little galaxy, and his hair and beard—they were both white as a cloud—trailed all the way down across his chest. His eyes were closed, and his hands were resting on his legs, which were folded up underneath him. He looked like he was meditating (which he does, all the time, in the stories—traveling to all kinds of spiritual planes and astral dimensions and *please* don't ask me to explain that because I'm not really sure what it means). "Wow," I said, "they must've spent a fortune on this!" And then I almost peed in my pants when the thought hit me that they wouldn't spend that kind of money just to promote a book. No, they must have actually made an Imaginalis *movie* and somehow kept it top secret and now—

The elephant man's eyes—the most incredible brown eyes I'd ever seen, with these super-deluxe long lashes—suddenly opened, and he looked *right at me*. What was weird and scary and exciting was that it didn't feel like some CGI image, it felt like a real living, breathing person (well, if you can call someone with a trunk and huge, floppy elephant ears a person) was really looking at *me*.

Like he could actually *see* me. "Dear sweet Mehera," the old elephant said, in a voice that was so gentle and loving that it made me feel happy just hearing it. "It's so wonderful to see you."

Without thinking, I answered, "It's great to see you, too, Lord Nossyss." (In the books, almost everyone calls him *Lord* Nossyss. Only Prince Imagos gets to call him Uncle.) As soon as I said it, I felt like a complete moron, talking to a CGI character on a YouTube page.

"No, no, dear one," he answered, "you must call me *Uncle*. After all, we're old friends, you and I."

My mouth fell open. "Wait, wait, wait," I said. "That's—that's impossible."

"What's impossible?" Uncle Nossyss asked.

"You're talking to me." No one, I thought, could come up with a computer program like that, no matter how big their budget was . . . could they?

"Of course I am," the elephant answered. "But Mehera, creating a soul mirror like this requires a very high, and very delicate, order of magic. This place makes it difficult to sustain a—"

"That's *impossible!*" I said again.

Uncle Nossyss waved his trunk at me. "I thought we'd already established that," he said. "Now, listen, Mehera, time is short. I need you to build the Bridge."

"How are you *doing* this?"

He ignored my question. "The Prince is depending on you," he said. "We're all depending on you. Build the Bridge, Mehera. The Unbelievable Bridge. It's the only thing that can save us."

"This—this has got to be a trick," I said. Don't ask me what *kind* of trick, because I had no clue.

Uncle Nossyss sighed. "I'd hoped to avoid this," he said—and then the old elephant closed his eyes, wrinkled up his forehead like he was concentrating with all his might, and *pushed his trunk through the computer screen*—moving through the glass like it was made out of water. I felt his trunk—*actually felt it*—for just a second as it touched my cheek. Then the trunk pulled quickly back, and Uncle Nossyss got kind of wobbly, like what he'd just done had been incredibly hard and he didn't have much strength left at all. "Did that," Nossyss said, and he was having a hard time catching his breath, "feel like a trick to you?"

I grabbed onto the side of her desk, afraid that I was going to faint. I mean a for-real, flat-on-my-back, out-like-a-light faint. I thought my brains were going to blow out of the top of my head or maybe melt right out of my ears. Which is why I did what any other kid would have done in the same situation: I screamed for my father. Really loud. "*Paaaaaaaaapaaa!*"

Papa, who'd been downstairs reading, charged into the room, all red-faced and out of breath. "What is it, Mehera? What's wrong?"

I couldn't talk. Just pointed to the computer screen. "What, goose?" Papa asked.

"Do you," I finally croaked, "see that?"

Papa looked at the monitor. "Sure," he said. "I can see it." He turned back to me, confused. "But I don't—"

"Wh-what," I stammered. "What d-do you see?"

Papa stared at the monitor, confused. "It's a YouTube video," he said. "But there's nothing in it."

There sure *was* something in it: a talking elephant whose voice sounded weak all of a sudden, like it was hard to get the words out. "Mehera . . . I can't keep the soul mirror open much longer. . . ."

"You heard that, right?" I asked my father.

"All I can hear is crackling," he said. "All I can see are"—he squinted—"wiggly lines."

"And that's all?"

"Of course that's all," Uncle Nossyss said, and he had the same kind of impatient tone Papa gets when I've been asking him the same question four or five hundred times in a row. (I do that sometimes.) "He doesn't see the way you do, he doesn't hear the way you do. Now *send him away*." (He sounded frustrated . . . not with me,

I don't think. It was more like he was frustrated with the situation, if you know what I mean.)

"Mehera Bea," Papa said, holding my face in his hands, "what is going on?"

"I think," I said, my eyes moving from Papa to Uncle Nossyss and back again, "I must've fallen asleep while I was sitting here. I must've . . . had a bad dream or—"

Papa smiled and kissed my forehead. "You had me worried there for a minute." He kissed me again. "What've I always told you, goose? Dreams aren't real, and they can't hurt you." He got up. "It's getting late, sweetie. Go to bed, okay?" He headed for the door, stopped a moment, then turned. "Wanna take out the mat and sleep on my floor? Like the old days?"

I almost said yes, I *wanted* to say yes, but I couldn't. I had to figure this out. "No," I answered. "But thanks, Papa. I'll take a rain check, okay?"

He smiled back. I could tell the rain-check part made him happy. "Sounds good," he said, then left the room.

I swiveled around in my chair, turned back to the image on the screen—it was all blurry now—in time to hear Uncle Nossyss say four final words: "Build the Unbelievable Bridge." Then the browser suddenly quit, and no matter how many times I clicked on the YouTube link, I couldn't get the page, or the old elephant, back again.

CHAPTER TEN
The Choice

I shut down the computer, went over to my bed, climbed in, and pulled the covers over my head. He touched me, I thought. I felt it. My mind was all jumbled up, my hands were shaking. My eyes—and don't ask me why, I have no clue—were all wet, like I was going to start bawling. How could an image on a screen . . . touch me?

I stayed there, under the covers, for more than an hour, trying to figure out what had happened. But there was no way I *could* figure it. No way any of it made sense—not unless I *had* fallen asleep at the computer and dreamed it. But if I had, why was Uncle Nossyss still there, still talking to me, after my father came into the room, when I was totally wide-awake? Well, there was one other answer, one that scared me more than I'd ever been scared before: What if, I wondered, I'm totally crazy? What if I've completely lost my mind? Then I remembered how they always say on television that if you *think* you've lost your mind, you haven't. But that was TV, right, and this was real life.

I felt so weird . . . and kind of scared, too . . . that I thought about going into my father's room and taking him up on his offer to sleep on the floor. But I was afraid that if I told Papa about Uncle Nossyss, he'd think I really *was* crazy and have me sent away to some kind of Asylum for Unstable Tweens Who Talk to Fictional People. (Look, I know my father would never do that, but that night, I wasn't sure about *anything*.)

I pushed back the covers, just a little, looked over at the computer to see if there was anything *strange* going on over there—there wasn't, thank God—and then crawled halfway off the bed, reaching over to grab an old photo album from my bookshelf. I hadn't looked at it in years—in fact, I'd almost forgotten it was there—but, that night, I knew, I just knew, that it was exactly what I needed.

I'd found the album when I was eight or so, digging around in my parents' bedroom. It was filled with pictures of Mama and Papa before I was born, some of them from before they were even married. The photographs inside were so old that some of the colors were fading, but something about them always seemed new to me, like they'd just been taken yesterday. When I was a kid I used to look at it all the time, laughing at my father's bushy hair—I think I like him better bald—and trying to figure out if my mother and I looked alike. Papa says we do, but I'm not really sure. I mean, Mama was *beautiful*, and no one would ever call me that, not even Andrew Suarez.

My favorite pictures were from a trip my parents took to India—a long time ago, back in 1980-something, when they were still in college. There was something so magical about the women in their colorful saris and the ancient temples and, especially, the statues of those amazing Hindu gods. But I think the best part about those India pictures was how happy my mother looked. Papa said she'd waited her whole life to go to India— she'd been dreaming about it since she was a kid—and the only time he ever saw her as happy was when *I* was born. I found out later that Papa'd *hated* India as much as Mama'd loved it. "Believe me," he told me, "you haven't pooped till you've pooped in a hole in the ground while ants crawl up your legs." The only reason he went was because it meant so much to Mama, which, when you think about it, is incredibly sweet. I once asked him if we could maybe go to India together one day, see all the places Mama loved. "Not in a million years," he said. "Not for a hundred million dollars." So I figured I'd wait till I was eighteen or nineteen—like Mama—and go by myself.

Back when I was a kid I'd sometimes do this totally goofy thing: sit with the album on my lap, close my eyes, and try to *think* myself into the pictures. I'd do it, too— well, in my imagination, at least. Find myself up walking along some street somewhere, holding my parents' hands. Or maybe snuggled up on a couch between them. I'd even have conversations with them—you know, in my mind.

And that night, sitting on the bed, looking at the photo album for the first time in years and years, I found myself doing the same thing. I was staring at this one picture of Mama in India. She was sitting in a rickshaw (that's sort of like a car and sort of like a motorcycle), her eyes all sparkling, smiling right at the camera, right at *me*—when all of a sudden, it felt like I was sitting there right next to her. Even weirder, I could hear her voice. "Don't forget, goose," she said, "always follow your dreams. They may not lead you where you expect to go—"

"But," I said out loud, finishing the thought, "they'll always lead you someplace wonderful." Mama used to say that to me *all the time* when I was little. There are a bunch of things about my mother that I've forgotten over the years—I guess it just kind of happens—but not that.

Okay, look, I knew I wasn't *really* in the picture, and I knew she wasn't really *talking* to me. It was just my imagination, some old memory creeping up from the back of my mind—but, really, it didn't matter, because just hearing those words again, I wasn't afraid anymore. Suddenly it didn't matter if Uncle Nossyss was real, a special effect, or proof that I was a total looney. All that mattered was that it had happened, that I'd seen him, talked to him. Sure, it was a mystery—bigger and better than any Nancy Drew had ever faced—but I was going to solve it. And I knew, right then, that the place to start was with his message. "Build the Bridge," the old elephant had said. "The Unbelievable Bridge."

I put the album down, reached back to the bookshelf, and grabbed the second Imaginalis novel. One chapter of *The World Below* told the story of an ancient kingdom that existed long before Imaginalis (which was supposed to be older than time, so don't ask me how that worked). Old Imaginalis—that's what the Imaginalian historians, the Historigicians, called it, because no one knew its real name—was ruled by a winged Queen, with silver skin, who—well, here's how Mrs. Morice-Gilland said it.

The Silver Queen presided over an Age of Miracles more magnificent than any ever seen on any world, in any time, in any universe. But something terrible happened—a great disaster that not even the seers of Old Imaginalis could foretell—and the kingdom fell.

As her kingdom crashed around her, the Queen created a bridge, constructed from her deepest dreams and desires; from her faith in the magic of the impossible and her belief in the unbelievable. The Silver Queen sent that bridge—the Unbelievable Bridge, she called it—from the center of her heart, out across the Ten Million Intersecting Universes, to a newborn world on the far side of Infinity. With her dying breath, the Queen dispatched the souls of her people to that new world, scattered them across the land like seeds. Over time, they were reborn as trees and oceans, mountains and valleys. Strange and wondrous animals. Handsome magicians. Beautiful enchantresses. And the day finally came when all the creatures that populated that young world gathered to name it. And they called their home Imaginalis.

I'd always loved the idea of the Unbelievable Bridge, and when I wrote my own Imaginalis stories, I used the Bridge as a way for my main character—who just happened to be named Mehera Beatrice Crosby—to cross over from Earth to Imaginalis. But those, I thought, were just stories. Or were they? I'd believed in Imaginalis with all my heart and all my soul since the night Papa started to read me the first book—but to believe *this much*? "No, no, no," I said out loud. "That's impossible."

But wasn't the impossible what the Imaginalis series was all about? Hadn't I told my entire class that Rajah Merogji's speech to Prince Imagos—when he explained how we're all trapped in "a prison of the possible"—was one of the greatest things I'd ever read? Well, here was a chance to see . . . *really see* . . . if that was true. Maybe this *was* some kind of dream, or maybe I was going a little (just a little) crazy. But maybe, I thought, it's more than that.

So I made up my mind to grab hold of the impossible and let my dreams lead me wherever they wanted to go. I fell asleep pretty fast after that, and when I woke up in the morning, I felt fantastic. It was like I'd slept for a whole year, the best sleep in the entire History of Sleeping.

The first thing I did the next morning was boot up my computer, but the emails from NOSSYSS were gone. I looked for the YouTube link, but that had disappeared, too—like it had never been there. Facebook? No messages on the wall. The next thing I did was check my phone, but most of the texts were from Celeste. I felt kind of bad (well, actually I felt totally guilty) that I'd been ignoring her—but I didn't text her back. I figured that, sooner or later, we'd work things out between us—okay, so I wasn't sure *how*—but right now I was heading for a place she could never understand: another world. The most amazing world ever. And it was waiting for me across the Unbelievable Bridge.

While I was brushing my teeth, Papa (who was getting ready to leave for the store) poked his head in the door. "You okay, goose?" he asked.

"Uh-huh," I answered, through a mouth full of toothpaste and spit.

"You sure?" he asked again.

"Uh-huh," I repeated. And I was. In some weird and scary and totally wonderful way, I was better than I'd ever been in my entire life.

CHAPTER ELEVEN
Across the Unbelievable Bridge

I sat in the old easy chair in the living room, flipped it back, stretched out my legs, and closed my eyes. This should be super easy, I thought. I'll do it just the way the Silver Queen did it in *The World Below*. The same way I did it in my stories. But I learned pretty quick that doing something in a story and doing it for real are two very different things. First thing I had to do was imagine the Unbelievable Bridge, see it there in my mind; but no matter how hard I tried, I just couldn't. In fact, I was seeing everything *but* the Bridge. After five or six minutes of trying so hard my head was starting to hurt, I suddenly realized that trying was the problem. In the books, Uncle Nossyss always liked to say that "The key to miracles isn't in the effort. It's in the *allowing*." Okay, so I was never exactly sure, but I kinda sorta *thought* that meant ignoring the part of yourself that wants to force

things to happen and letting another part of yourself . . .
something deeper and truer and, I guess, easier . . . take
over. For a second I got scared, but then I took a super-
deep breath, relaxed my body, relaxed my mind . . . and
allowed.

For a few minutes, all kinds of totally random thoughts
and feelings and images just sort of floated across my
mind, the same way they sometimes do before I fall
asleep. My father once told me the word that described
how that feels, and it's one I've always loved: hypnagogic.
So I hypnagoged along (and no, "hypnagogued" isn't a
word, but maybe it should be), letting my thoughts carry
me up, down, sideways, and over—and then, all of a
sudden, a gajillion images from the Imaginalis books
exploded in my head, running like scenes from a movie
that had been all mixed up and shown out of order. I
saw Prince Imagos and the Companions, all the magical
races and enchanted creatures, sky cities and under-
water kingdoms . . . and my heart just melted. It was
like every feeling I'd ever had during all the years I'd
been reading the Imaginalis books came back to me all
at once. I felt this big, warm burst of love for that whole
incredible world and for every single character—even
Pralaya. (Which was pretty weird. I mean, he's *the bad
guy*.) But there was something else I was feeling, too:
absolute belief. In Imaginalis . . . and in my own power

to get there. "Because it's impossible," I said out loud to myself, "I'll *do* it. Because it's unbelievable, *I'll believe.*" Without thinking, without trying—*just allowing*—I aimed for the impossible. Let all that belief just bubble up and explode out of my mind and—

I wasn't in my living room anymore. I was walking down my street—only it wasn't my street. It was kind of like the way things are in a dream, when they're familiar and not familiar at the same time. Only it was more real than any dream I'd ever had. All the houses were dark. The trees were like a hundred times bigger than normal; they seemed to stretch up into forever. And the sky: Even though the last I'd checked it was morning, it was somehow night now, and there were thousands, maybe even millions, of stars in the sky. And the stars and the trees all seemed *alive.* Not alive like they were breathing or moving or talking to me. No, alive because they seemed *aware* somehow. As if they knew themselves . . . and knew me . . . and they were happy I was there. Wherever There was. I kept walking for a few minutes . . . or it could have been a few days. Time, I realized, felt different, and it was impossible to tell one second from the next; they all seemed to kind of stretch apart and then melt back into one another.

And then I saw it up ahead, golden and glittering,

as wide as the whole world and tall as the sky. The Unbelievable Bridge. This may be hard to understand, but the Bridge was there and not there at the same time, like part of it was absolutely, totally real—as real as any bridge in the world—and another part was made of thoughts and feelings and all the imagination in the universe. More than just seeing it, I could feel it: hope and faith, trust and happiness, were shining out from the Unbelievable Bridge right into my heart. Spreading out into every single cell of my body.

Then I heard this voice—I couldn't tell if it was coming from inside my head or from the Bridge itself. "Mehera, hurry!" the voice said. "Mehera, they're waiting!"

And so I ran. I'm pretty lousy at sports—it takes me forever to run the mile when we do it in gym—but that day . . . or night . . . or whatever it was . . . I ran so fast I actually impressed myself. I jumped onto the deck of the Bridge—there was this really soft vibration, kind of like a warm current running up through my body, when I landed—and ran faster and faster, trying to figure out how, exactly, I was going to get across something that seemed to stretch out across the whole universe. Then—it was like my eyes were adjusting to the Unbelievable Bridge the same way they adjust to the dark—I started to see that the Bridge was splitting off in hundreds of different directions, into hundreds of different worlds. There were so many choices. So many places to go. But I knew, with all my heart, what place I was heading for: home. My *true* home.

And the second I thought that, there it was: Sheriar, the capital city of Imaginalis. It was still way far in the distance, but I could somehow see it all, in detail: glowing Transpheres, packed with people, sailing through the clouds kind of like flying buses. Gigantamundo towers reaching up into the sky. Banners and balloons. Festivals and parades. Music and laughter. Elephants and horses (some of were on all fours, but others were walking upright, on two legs). Then I caught a glimpse of the Rajah's palace, the most beautiful building I'd ever seen, sitting on top of a golden platform, in the middle of Amaram Lake. I'm not sure why, but I started laughing when I saw it. And running even faster.

There was no sign of the war, of all the damage Pralaya'd done. Every Imaginalian I saw looked happy, like they were all having the best day ever. That's when I realized that this wasn't any Imaginalis I'd ever read about. This was Imaginalis *after Imagos defeats Pralaya*. In the books, Prognostica, the Nebulous Seer, once predicted that Prince Imagos would rule over a Golden Age more spectacular than any since back when the Silver Queen was around. And I was going to be there to see it, to live it, to—

As fast as it appeared, Sheriar vanished—and the Unbelievable Bridge vanished, too. All of a sudden I was surrounded by darkness, everywhere I looked. It was blacker than any darkness I'd ever seen before and, even worse, it felt alive. Hungry. *Like it wanted to eat me.*

Something long and creepy—an octopus tentacle or maybe a giant cobra—slithered through that darkness, wrapped itself around my waist, and yanked me forward. I screamed—dumb as it sounds, I thought if I screamed loud enough, my father would come and save me—tried to push the snake creature . . . or whatever it was . . . off me. But the more I fought it, the tighter it had me. "Let me go!" I wailed.

"I will," a voice—a *familiar* voice—answered, "if you'll just stop struggling." A soft light suddenly appeared in front of me, pushing up through all that darkness, and I could *just* begin to make out two really big tusks, and then a face, staring at me with a little bit of annoyance and a whole lot of joy.

"Uncle Nossyss?" I cried.

"Yes, Mehera," the old elephant said, "it's me."

CHAPTER TWELVE
Nolandia

I realized that the light spinning in the middle of Nossyss's chest was his amulet and, as it got a little brighter, I could see him, *really* see him, standing there. This wasn't a YouTube video, this was the real thing.

"Close your mouth, Mehera," Uncle Nossyss said. "It's unbecoming."

I closed it, but in another two seconds it dropped open again. I mean, how could it not? I stood there gawking at every line in the old elephant's leathery face, every fluff of white hair, every wisp of his beard, every bulge in that ginormous belly. "It's really you," I finally said.

"I'm sorry if I startled you," Nossyss answered. "I knew that if I didn't act quickly, the tides would carry you away from us, possibly forever."

What I'd thought was a snake or an octopus had

actually been the old elephant's trunk, and now that I wasn't struggling, it was actually kind of cozy having it wrapped around me, carrying me along. It felt like we were ice skating—just kind of gliding through the dark—but with nothing, and I mean absolutely nothing, to see around us, it was hard to tell if we were really moving at all. "Tides?" I asked. "What do you mean? Where are we?"

"I think you know."

And, instantly, I did. "Nolandia!"

"Indeed," Nossyss said. One of his long, floppy ears lifted up, like he was listening for something. "You told your father that we were stuck in limbo—and, sadly, you were correct."

I had so many questions I didn't know where to start. "But how do you know what I told my father? And how did you get here? How did *I* get here?"

"Soon, Mehera, soon," Nossyss said. "But first let's find the others."

"The others?" I asked, so excited my voice was shaking. "You mean Prince Imagos and the Companions are—"

"You'll see for yourself," Uncle Nossyss said, but he didn't sound happy about it. "Soon enough."

* * *

We kept skating along through the darkness, with only the whirling light of Nossyss's amulet to guide us. But I wondered how it *could* guide us when we were sailing across a place that wasn't really a place, across a world that wasn't really a world. Still, Uncle Nossyss seemed to know where he was going, and really, he was Rajah Merogji's most trusted adviser and the wisest of all the wise men (if you could even call him a man) in Imaginalis, so if I couldn't trust him, who could I trust?

I started to ask a gazillion more questions, but the old elephant told me that he needed to concentrate if we were going to find the Companions' camp. "Nothing stays in one place very long here," he said. "It's very possible they've drifted off, without realizing it. And if we've lost them—" For just a second it sounded like he might actually be afraid. Like there was a chance we *could* lose them and the two of us would be stuck there in Nolandia forever, just skating around in the Nothing. "But, of course," he added quickly, trying to make me feel better (and maybe trying to make himself feel better, too), "we *will* find them."

In a few minutes—or a few hours or a few seconds, I sure couldn't tell—we did find them. Well, we found something: First thing I saw were these little glowing balls off in the distance, bobbing up and down in the air, and, as we got closer, I could see *something* moving in the light. A group of . . . well, I wasn't sure *what* they were. Long and gray and thin as silk, flapping around like curtains in front of an open window.

But they had eyes, too . . . just white slits, really . . . and mouths. Like shadows—if shadows were actually alive. "We're not going that way, are we?" I asked Uncle Nossyss. He didn't answer, just kept moving toward the shadows—and I guess that was my answer.

If I could have, I would have run the other way, but in Nolandia "the other way" doesn't really *mean* anything— and I figured I had a better chance of getting home in one piece if I stuck with Uncle Nossyss, even if it meant getting up close and personal with those Shadow Thingies. As we got nearer to them, I could see that there were at least two people there who didn't look like shadows at all. In fact, they looked totally human (well, more or less) and totally *familiar*. So familiar my heart started pounding away in my chest and it was all I could do not to burst out crying.

First, there was this woman, maybe five feet tall, with thick golden hair that was falling all around her in knots and braids and curls and kinks, totally covering her face and body. The only reason I could even tell it *was* a woman was because I could see her arms and hands—and a little bit of her feet, too—and they were so small, so . . . delicate, I guess is the word . . . that there was no way it could have been a man under there. Plus, anyone who'd read Mrs. Morice-Gilland's stories would've known right away who it was: Prognostica, the Nebulous Seer, one of my favorite characters in all the Imaginalis books. I was so happy to see her, I almost started laughing. (But I didn't. It would have been disrespectful.)

And then there was the boy. Well, I'm calling him a boy, but the truth is, he wasn't like any boy I'd ever seen before. Sure, he looked like he was maybe fifteen or sixteen, but he didn't slouch there with his shoulders hanging down or with some stupid expression on his face (y'know, trying really hard to be tough or cool) like the guys at my school. He stood there like . . . well, like he was *born* to stand there. And was he ever handsome— with this gorgeous brown skin and these big, sad eyes and beautiful black hair falling in ringlets across his shoulders. There was a quiver filled with arrows—and not just any arrows; these were the Eternity Arrows— across his back, and he wore a golden crown, with a snake head made of rubies at the top and a diamond spider dangling down in the front. But even without the crown I would've known, the second I saw him, that this was

Prince Imagos, only son of Rajah Merogji. Heir to the throne of Imaginalis. Soon as I got a good look at him, I suddenly remembered all the goofy stories I'd written . . . the ones where I saved the kingdom and kinda sorta kissed the Prince and maybe even married him at the end . . . and I felt so totally embarrassed that I would have crawled into a hole if I could have found one.

"Oh, Uncle, you brought her," Prognostica said, rushing toward us. "Just as I predicted you would!" (Imagine a flute that can talk and you'll have an idea of what she sounded like. It was the most beautiful voice I'd ever heard.)

Uncle Nossyss put me down—I couldn't really see the ground, but it felt all squishy and swampy—and the Nebulous Seer kissed me on both cheeks. I thought about curtsying to her or maybe bowing, but I was so excited I just started jumping up and down. "Prognostica!" I shouted. "I can't believe it's really you!"

"Yes, dear, it's me," Prognostica said, taking my hands in hers and looking into my eyes. (Well, I could only guess about that: the Nebulous Seer's eyes were totally hidden by *all that hair*—but it sure felt like she was looking at me.) "And I'm so, so, *so* delighted to meet you. Come," she went on, hooking her arm through mine, "let me introduce you to His Highness."

I turned to face Prince Imagos—or tried to. After about a second, I couldn't take it and stared down at the tips of my Doc Martens. "Your Majesty," I said, squeaking like a mouse.

"A pleasure, Mehera," he said. His voice was a little higher than I'd imagined, like it hadn't quite changed yet. "I only wish it was under happier circumstances."

I looked around. "Where are the others?" I asked.

"Others?"

"The rest of the Companions," I said. "Shokra and Natu and Wallawalla and—"

The Prince shook his head and sighed. "We three are all who remain," he said. "At least . . . in this form."

"This form?" I said. The Shadow Thingies moved closer to us, gathering around the Prince, and my skin just started to crawl. My stomach turned upside down, and I thought I was going to be sick. "You—you don't mean that *they*—?"

"Are all that is left of the people of Imaginalis," the Prince answered.

I looked from the Prince to Prognostica to Nossyss. "But you three aren't shadows. You—"

"We have only maintained these forms," the Prince said, "because of you."

"*Me?*"

"Your belief in us," Prince Imagos answered, "runs deep. Sustains us, Mehera. The others—" His voice trailed off, and the Shadow Thingies floated back . . . swallowed up into the darkness around us.

I looked right at Imagos again—for a couple of seconds, at least. There was something in his eyes . . . and this might sound a little weird . . . that reminded me of my mother. She was the kind of person who really tried to treat everyone the same. Didn't matter if you were the president of the United States or someone coming in to Queenstown Family for a free breakfast. Mama thought everybody should be treated with kindness and respect. (And, believe me, that's not very easy. I know because I've tried it.) I could tell that Prince Imagos was the same way. He may have been the heir to the throne and all that, but he didn't think he was better than me or anyone else. "How," I squeaked, then cleared my throat, "how do you know my name? You *all* know me. How is that possible?" All of a sudden I was sure this had to be some kind of crazy dream. There was no way it could be real. "How is *any* of this possible?"

Prince Imagos looked over at the old elephant. "Lord Nossyss will explain," he said. "But please, Uncle"—he tried to hide it, but I could tell he was really worried—"don't take too long."

CHAPTER THIRTEEN
A Song of Hope

We were sitting in a circle, those glowing balls of light—they were called mindfires, because *they were actually made from people's thoughts*—bobbing up and down in front of us, casting this beautiful glow over everyone's faces. Well, everyone human. Those Shadow Thingies were flapping around in a wind that I couldn't even feel, totally creeping me out.

Prognostica—I had the feeling she could sense what I was thinking (or maybe she just saw the spooked look on my face)—put a hand on my arm. "Don't fear them, dear," she said. "They can't help what they've become."

I had a ton of questions about how this had all happened, but, when I started to ask, Imagos waved me down. "Let Nossyss talk," he said. He didn't say it in a mean or bossy way or anything, but he said it like a prince, like someone who was used to having people obey him—and so I shut up pretty quick. I wasn't one of his subjects, so it's not like I *had* to do what he said, but the truth is I wanted to. It made me feel like one of them. Like an Imaginalian.

"As you've long suspected," Uncle Nossyss began, talking directly to me, "as you've long *believed*, Imaginalis isn't just some story in a book. *Imaginalis is real.* But what you don't know is that there is a link—old and deep and true—between your Earth and our world. A spark of connection that burns brightly in your heart, Mehera. I've spent years studying the old scroll fragments—"

"And," the Nebulous Seer said, "consulting with *me*. My visions can see backward into the past as well as forward into the future." Okay, so she sounded like she was bragging. But only a little. And if I could see into the future and the past, I'd brag, too.

Uncle Nossyss smiled at Prognostica. "You've been a great help," he told her, and then went on with his story. "You know, of course, about the Silver Queen and Old Imaginalis. My studies have led me to theorize that, when the First Empire fell, not all of the Silver Queen's seeds took root in Imaginalian soil. I believe that some took root on *your* world, Mehera. In the hearts of a fortunate few—a tree here, a river there, a fish, a beast, a human—who, without even realizing it, carried the imprint of Imaginalis in their souls. And passed it down from generation to generation to generation, over endless cycles of time."

I tried to keep my big mouth shut, but I just couldn't. "You mean," I said, "that I'm—"

"Imaginalian?" Nossyss answered. "No." He ran his trunk across my cheek. (I guess he could see how disappointed I was.) "You are not one of us, Mehera—but you are *attuned* to us. Vibrating *with* us." Okay, so that wasn't as good as actually being an Imaginalian, but I liked it just the same. "There are," Nossyss went on, "very few left on Earth who still hold the Silver Queen's charge. But you do. And that's why you never doubted our existence. That's why you've always believed. You . . . and the Dreamer."

"The Dreamer?" I asked.

"The one who didn't just feel Imaginalis but saw it, breathed it, put it to paper, and dreamed it alive."

"Mrs. Morice-Gilland!" I shouted (maybe a little too loud).

"Mrs. Morice-Gilland," Uncle Nossyss answered—and the way he said her name, well, you could tell that he . . . that all the Imaginalians . . . looked up to her. Thought she was something incredible.

Truth is, I felt kind of jealous of that. I guess a part of me wanted to be the only one on Earth with this special connection to Imaginalis. But it only took a second—or two—for me to realize that sharing something like this with the Greatest Writer in the History of Writing is a pretty wonderful thing. "Is she here?" I asked, looking around, hoping maybe I'd finally get to meet her. "Is she coming?"

"No," Uncle Nossyss said, with a confused look on his face. "It's been most . . . frustrating. I've searched and searched, but I've been unable to locate her. She's been . . . hidden from me somehow." He smiled then. "But we are fortunate indeed, Mehera, to have found you. For you, I believe, have the power to carry us out of Nolandia."

"Me? *How?*"

"First," the Prince said, "explain to Mehera how we came to be here."

Nossyss sat for a moment, thinking, and then said one word: "Pralaya."

"Pralaya?" I said. "*He* trapped you here? Well, that figures, right? Dirty, rotten, no-good—"

"I see no need," a voice said, "to insult me."

One shape separated itself from the rest of the Shadow Thingies. It floated and flapped around me for a few seconds, like it was checking me out. Then it started to change, really slow, kind of like a picture coming into focus, taking on more of a human form until it finally became a man. Well, maybe I should call him a ghost—because I could see right through him. His skin was as white as Lord Nossyss's tusks, but he was really handsome (not anywhere near as handsome as Imagos, of course) and really tall, with long red hair flowing down his back and the bluest eyes I'd ever seen. He was wearing silk robes and a gazillion jewels and had this jade crown on his head that must've been three feet high. And he reeked, *totally reeked*, of perfume, like he'd tossed ten bottles all over himself. But all the perfume in the world couldn't cover up the fact that there was something . . . *wrong* about this man (or ghost or *whatever* he was). That's the best way I can put it: Everything about him was just plain wrong.

I knew right away that this was Pralaya.

"You look troubled, Mehera," he said, floating slowly toward me. "Does my form not please you? I have thousands, you know. Male, female, young, old, in any color, any shape you'd like. Just take your pick and—"

Before Pralaya could get another word out, there was this roar (so loud it nearly blew out my eardrums)—and that's when I realized that there was a *lion thing* standing next to him. At first I got pretty scared, because I thought it was one of the creatures in Pralaya's army of monsters (according to the books, he's got a hundred thousand monsters, from a hundred thousand nether-worlds, serving him), but then I saw the wings spreading out from the lion's back and the human face—a *nice* face, too—underneath the mane. That's when I knew this had to be Yalee, friend and protector of every rajah since Imaginalis was born. "Do not," the lion snarled to Pralaya, "go anywhere near that child."

"I was just paying my respects," Pralaya said, floating back and hovering there at the edge of the circle.

Then Yalee turned toward me—bowed his head, nuzzled his mane against me, so close I could actually smell his breath. Celeste has a golden retriever named Ozma, and she's totally adorable, but her breath could make you puke for a week. You'd figure a lion's breath would be ten times worse, right? But not Yalee's. His was actually sweet, kind of like lilacs. "An honor to meet you, Mehera," the lion said.

"An honor to meet you, too," I answered. Only it didn't feel like an honor. I was so frightened I was shaking. Which doesn't make any sense. I mean, Yalee's one of the good guys, right? But he only shows up in a few of the books (and not for very long, either) so I guess I didn't feel comfortable with him the way I did with the others.

Plus, *he was a lion*. (I remember going to the circus with my parents when I was four or five, and the second the lions came out, I started crying and shrieking and we had to leave, right in the middle of the show.)

I think Yalee could sense how I was feeling, because he smiled and backed away, settling down beside Pralaya. I realized then that the lion was *guarding* Pralaya. You could see from the way he was sitting there that he was all ready to pounce at the first sign of trouble. In the books, Yalee had actually killed Pralaya—and *eaten* him—twice. Okay, so Pralaya managed to cast some ancient spell and come back to life, but I could tell from the way the magician looked at the lion that he was more afraid of him than I was.

I pointed at Pralaya. "I don't get it," I said. "Why's he even here with you?"

"Pralaya," Prince Imagos answered, "is as trapped here as the rest of us. Enemy or not, he is Imaginalian and belongs with his people." He cleared his throat. "Now tell her, Uncle, how this all came to be."

"It began," Uncle Nossyss said, "when Prince Imagos returned to Sheriar and amassed a formidable army. Preparing to seize the capital city, he—"

"Wait, wait," I said, "that's not in any of the books."

Nossyss smiled. "Our lives go on, Mehera, whether

the books continue or not."

"Right," I said, feeling like a total moron. "So that means you were pretty much at the end of the story. Ready to take back Sheriar . . . and the throne?"

"We'll never know," Imagos said, "if it was truly the end, because—"

"Because," Pralaya interrupted, gliding forward again (Yalee right behind him), "I built a weapon. What, on your world, would be called a . . . bomb. But mine was not a creation of technology." He grinned—but there was nothing happy about it. In fact, he looked kind of demented. "Mine was built on sorcery, tapping into the energy of Nolandia itself. Call it a *Nothing Bomb*: guaranteed to erase any opponent from existence, utterly and irreversibly." The grin suddenly slipped away. "But there were a few . . . problems."

"Yes," Uncle Nossyss said, whirling to face Pralaya, waving his trunk at him. "Your wretched bomb didn't destroy just your enemies! It sucked all of Imaginalis into Nolandia! Every man, woman, and child! Even your own followers!" He pointed to the Shadow Thingies. "Look, Mehera," he went on. "Look at what the monster has done to us! It's—" And then Nossyss got this look on his face, like he was suddenly more angry at himself for losing control than he was at Pralaya. He closed his eyes, took a really long, really deep, breath. "I'm sorry, my Prince," he said, bowing his head.

"Even you," the Prince answered, with a sad smile, "are allowed a little anger now and then, Uncle."

The old elephant nodded and went on with his story. "The weapon detonated prematurely," he said. "Pralaya was caught in the heart of the blast—and so—"

"And so," Pralaya said (changing from a ghost to a Shadow Thingy and back again), "I was the first to be ripped out of Imaginalis and hurled into Nolandia. And I will be the first to be consumed by this place. Bled away, like swiftly vanishing smoke, into this damned endless darkness."

"You're *dying*?" I asked. I actually felt sorry for him—and I hated myself for it. Here was this totally evil creature who'd destroyed all of Imaginalis. Why should I care if he lived or died?

"We're all dying," Uncle Nossyss said. "No . . . worse than dying: We're *undying*. In the end, every last one of us will be dissolved into the nothing. And when that happens, all traces of our world will be erased. No one will remember we ever existed."

"*I'll* remember," I said.

"No, Mehera, you won't," Prince Imagos said, walking over to me. "Because once we're gone from here"—he pointed to the darkness all around us—"we'll be gone from *there*"—he touched my head— "too."

"I won't let that happen!" I said. I know it was a stupid thing to do, but I grabbed the Prince's hands (they were ice-cold, and that surprised me): I guess I just wanted to make him feel better. It took me about two seconds to realize that you don't just go around grabbing princes like that, and I was about to let go when I got a good look at Imagos's hands and saw that the light of the mindfires was *actually passing through them.* "You, too?" I said, horrified.

"All of us," the Prince whispered. His voice suddenly sounded different. Like he wasn't in front of me at all. Like he was an echo—from someplace really far away. "All of us," he repeated.

For a second the whole group started to flicker, kind of like a fire that was dying out, and I was terrified that they'd all vanish right then and there. "I won't let you go," I said. "You're too important to me. You matter too much, and *I won't let you go.*"

That's when Prognostica started to sing—a sweet, gentle song that didn't have any words (well, not any that I understood)—and something in the music seemed to help the Companions become more solid. It was like every note gave them—gave *all* of us—hope. Even the Shadow

Thingies seemed calmer now. Like they believed, if only for a little while, that things were going to get better.

"That's beautiful," I said when the Nebulous Seer was done.

"The singing was mine, dear," Prognostica said, "but the inspiration came from you."

"Me?"

"And that, sweet Mehera," the old elephant said, "is why I risked all, pushed my magic to its very limit, to find you and call you here." Grunting, Nossyss pushed himself to his feet. "You believe in us even more than we believe in ourselves. And that belief will lead us over the Bridge to freedom."

"You want *me* to take you back to Imaginalis?" I asked.

As soon as I said that, the Prince got this look on his face like his heart had just broken into a zillion pieces. I looked over at Uncle Nossyss, but he turned his head away. "What is it?" I asked Prognostica.

She didn't answer for a few seconds and then, in a voice so soft and sad it almost made me cry, said, "There is no Imaginalis to go home to."

CHAPTER FOURTEEN
The Escape

"What?" I said. I couldn't believe what I was hearing.

"Let me show you," Prognostica answered, an arm pushing out from all that hair. Her fingers pressed against my forehead. "Close your eyes and look," Prognostica whispered.

"Don't you mean *open* my eyes and look?"

"*Close* them," she insisted.

I did what she said, and just like that, I wasn't in Nolandia anymore. I was in Sheriar, the capital city of Imaginalis. But this wasn't Sheriar the way I'd seen it from the Unbelievable Bridge or read about it in the books. This was like some ancient ruin, ten million years old. All the great towers had fallen and turned to dust. Amaram Lake had dried up. And the people . . .

they were all just sort of standing there, looking confused, almost hypnotized—like they couldn't remember who they were, *where* they were.

And then, all of a sudden, I heard thunder—so loud I couldn't stand it—and it started to rain. Only it *wasn't* rain, not any kind of rain I'd ever seen before: thick oily gobs of blackness—*pieces of Nolandia*, I realized (or maybe Prognostica put the thought in my head)—came pouring down, oozing over the ruins, overflowing the lake, rushing through the streets like a humongous black tidal wave. Inch by inch, the city was being swallowed up in that darkness, and I knew that soon the darkness would be the only thing left.

And then the wave started moving toward me, so fast I knew I could never get out of its way. I threw my hands over my face and screamed.

"Open your eyes, Mehera," Prognostica said. "Open your eyes *now*."

I did—and I was back in Nolandia. But I knew I could never forget what I saw, what I felt. *What Pralaya did.* "He—he destroyed everything," I said to Prognostica.

Pralaya floated toward us, with Yalee at his heels. "It was not," he said quietly, "my intention. Why would I destroy the very kingdom I was born to rule? It was the weapon. The power was too great. I should never have—"

He went from a ghost to a shadow, from a shadow to just a swirl of black smoke. "I'm sorry," he whispered—and, for a second, I actually believed him. But then I remembered what a liar Pralaya was—and how he'd always use those lies to get people to do exactly what he wanted. You couldn't trust anything that miserable creep said or did.

Imagos stood up, facing us all. "Imaginalis is denied us now," he said. "We cannot look back."

"But I *saw* it," I said. "Saw Sheriar . . . when I came over the Bridge. Everything was wonderful. It was perfect. It was—"

"You saw," the Prince said, turning to me, "what your heart *wanted* to see."

"Then what are you going to do?" I whined.

"Why," Imagos answered, smiling, "we're going with you."

"With me?" I said.

"Do you see any other alternative?" the Prince asked. "Our home is denied us, this world will consume us. But your world . . . your world is the world of hope."

"My world?" I said. "Do you have any idea what it's like back there in the CNN Reality? We've got wars going on all the time and people *starving* . . . and . . . and diseases and global warming and—"

"Is that what your life is like?" Uncle Nossyss asked.

"Mine? No. I'm . . . I guess I'm one of the lucky ones." Which was true. Considering how rough life is for so many people—like the ones who come into Queenstown Family every week—I really *was* lucky. So how come I didn't I feel that way? How come the idea of going back home made me feel kind of sick to my stomach?

Uncle Nossyss looked at me. Well, it felt more like he looked *into* me. "No matter our circumstances," he said, "our pain is our pain. Our loss is our loss." I wasn't sure, but it was almost like his mind was kind of poking around *inside* mine, pushing down deep into some places that . . . well, I wasn't sure *what* they were. And I didn't want to know. Ever.

"The only way back," I said, "is over the Unbelievable Bridge, and the Bridge—is gone."

"Not gone," Nossyss said. He tapped my forehead with his trunk. "It's in there still. Nolandia simply made it invisible, but you . . . you can bring it back. Carry us to safety."

"All of you?" I asked. The Shadow Thingies started flapping around like they were caught in a hurricane, making this awful wailing sound.

"No, not all of us," Prince Imagos said. "Once we're

safe on your world, we'll find a way to restore them. Restore Imaginalis." He turned to the Shadow Thingies. "In my father's name, I swear it," he said—and the *way* he said it, I don't think anyone could doubt him. The shadows quieted down. I could feel—or at least I thought I did—how much they believed in their Prince. *I* believed in him, too. How could I not? Ever since I was seven years old, Imagos had been my hero—Harry Potter, King Arthur, Peter Pan, and Superman all rolled into one—and I believed with all my heart that he was going to lead his people home.

"Enough of this!" Pralaya shouted, spinning like a tornado now, whirling into the air over our heads. "Build the Bridge, girl! Get us out of this miserable place!"

"You," Imagos said to Pralaya, "aren't going anywhere." Pralaya rushed toward the Prince, but one warning look, one soft growl, from the lion, and he backed away. "You will remain here, under Yalee's watchful eye."

"Left here," Pralaya howled, "to fade into oblivion!"

"We will return for *them*," Prince Imagos said, pointing to the Shadow Thingies, "and we will return for *you*, Pralaya." Then Imagos turned back to me, folded his arms across his chest. "The Unbelievable Bridge," he commanded. "*Now.*"

* * *

"Mehera? Mehera, honey?"

"Huh?" I jumped up in the chair and looked around, not sure if I was awake or asleep, in Queenstown or Nolandia. "Am I back?" I asked. "Are they here?"

"Whoa, whoa, goose, take it easy," Papa said. "Back from where? Is who here?"

Papa had this super-deluxe worried look on his face. "You okay, Mehera Bea?" he asked, touching my forehead to see if I had a fever. "You feeling all right?"

I looked around the family room, realizing where I was and that Papa and I were the only ones there, and my heart just kind of fell through the floor. "It was a dream," I groaned. "The whole thing was a stupid dream."

Papa felt my head again. "Are you *sure* you're okay?"

I was about to say something rude that I'd only have to apologize for later when there was this humongazoid flash of light, and then the entire house shook so hard that I actually tumbled out of my chair and fell flat on the floor.

When I looked up, Prince Imagos, Uncle Nossyss, and Prognostica were standing in front of me.

CHAPTER FIFTEEN
The New World

My father just kind of stood there, staring at the Companions, then stopped for a second, scratched his head, and turned to me. "Papa," I said, "I can explain!" Actually I couldn't—not without sounding completely nutsoid—but I was willing to give it a try.

"Get up, Mehera," Papa said, reaching down and helping me to my feet. "I was *really* hoping you were done with this fainting routine," he whispered.

"Fainting?" I said. "I wasn't fainting. I fell out of the chair when they came over the Bridge. I'm surprised the whole house didn't just split in half. I mean, it felt like an earthquake, didn't it?"

"Earthquake?" Papa said. "Mehera, what are you talking about?" He was about to say something else—something annoyingly parental—but stopped himself.

"We can talk about this later, okay?" he went on, whispering again. "We don't have to get into this discussion in front of your friends." He turned to Prince Imagos and the others. "So," he said to me, "aren't you going to introduce us?"

"You want me to introduce you?" I asked. He's sounding awfully calm, I thought, considering the aliens who just crash-landed in our living room.

"Of course I do," Papa replied. He walked over to Prince Imagos, reached out, and shook his hand. "Clifford Crosby," he said. "And you are—?"

"Papa, no!" I said, throwing myself between my father and the Prince. "You don't just walk up to him and shake his hand like he's a regular person!"

"I don't?"

"No! For crying out loud, Papa, he's a prince. The son of Rajah Merogji. Heir to the throne of Imagin—"

"Okay, Mehera," Uncle Nossyss said. "You can stop now."

"Stop what?"

"Just because *we* love to pretend that we're characters from the Imaginalis books doesn't mean that we have to bother your father with our little game."

"*Excuse* me?" I said.

Nossyss walked over to Papa and said, "My name is Ellison Funt."

"It *is?*" I yelped.

"I'm in your daughter's French class."

"You *are?*"

Uncle Nossyss squinted at me and then gave me a little whap on the top of my head with his trunk. "*Yes. I. Am.*" He turned back to face Papa, and that's when I saw that the amulet on his chest was spinning like crazy now, lights sparking and jumping all over the place. Papa's eyes kind of glazed over, his mouth was hanging open, and he had an incredibly stupid smile on his face.

"Hey," I said, suddenly worried, "what'd you do to him?"

"He's fine," Nossyss said, "but I needed to distract him a moment so I can explain."

"Explain what?"

Nossyss pointed to the others. "Look," he said—and I did. Imagos and Prognostica weren't there. Except they were. Kind of. The Prince was wearing a Star Wars T-shirt, a pair of faded old jeans and red high-top sneakers. Instead of his crown, there was a sideways baseball cap sitting on his head. Next to Imagos was this blond girl—she was maybe eleven or twelve—in a bright yellow dress, with two stiff pigtails sticking straight out from the sides of her head, and bangs (and, boy, did she ever need to trim them) flopping over her eyes. I knew that had to be Prognostica.

When I turned back to Uncle Nossyss, I saw that he—well, "Ellison Funt," which was as goofy a name as I'd ever heard—wasn't an elephant anymore. He was a short, tubby kid of about thirteen, with a big grin and this ginormous nose, wearing a shirt that was way too large, pants that were way too tight, and shoes that must have been size sixteen. I couldn't help myself; I laughed. Hysterically.

"It was the best," Ellison Funt said, "that I could do on the spur of the moment."

"So that's what my *dad* sees?" I asked.

"A wonderful idea, Uncle," Imagos said. "This way we can blend in with the locals. I commend you."

"How long," Prognostica asked, "will we be trapped in these odd forms?" Considering what she usually looked like, I didn't think she looked *that* odd.

"The form," Nossyss said, "is an illusion." He snapped his fat fingers, and the Companions were back in their Imaginalian bodies. "Beneath the veil of illusion, you remain exactly as you've always been." He snapped again, and they were normal—okay, maybe normal's the wrong word—Earth kids again. "It's only the humans who see you this way."

I realized that I could see the Companions in all their forms: Tilt my head one way, they were human; tilt it another and they were Imaginalian. Which I thought was pretty cool. "Speaking of humans," I said, pointing to my father. A big, fat trail of drool was oozing from the corner of Papa's mouth. His eyes were starting to cross. "Could you unvoodoo my dad?" I walked over to Papa and pushed his mouth closed. "He's not perfect, but he's the only one I've got."

Once he was unvoodooed, Papa was really happy to meet my new friends. Ellison introduced Imagos as Sonny Royal and Prognostica as Claire Voyante, and even though the names were totally ridiculous (or maybe it was another of Uncle Nossyss's spells), Papa didn't seem suspicious in the least. Ellison told Papa that they were Imaginalis fans and we'd all met at a new fantasy book club at the school.

"Why didn't you *tell* me about this?" Papa asked me. He was so thrilled I'd found some new friends that I felt kind of guilty not telling him the truth. But, hey, they *were* my new friends, weren't they, and we *were* all fans of Imaginalis. Just not in the way he thought. He invited the three of them to stay for dinner, "if it's okay with your parents" (guess what—it was), and cooked up a huge pot of pasta, then panfried it in garlic, olive oil, onions, and fresh tomatoes—just the way I love it. The

Imaginalians all seemed to enjoy it—especially Ellison, who ate three bowls.

Later Papa went up to his room to read and the four of us went out into the backyard to make our plans. "First of all," I said, "we've gotta figure out where you're gonna stay. We don't really have a lot of room in the house, and besides, my dad would *never* let boys stay overnight, and anyway, what happens when he asks what time your *parents* are gonna pick you up?"

"Don't worry about that," Uncle Nossyss said. "We'll stay in the tree house."

"Great idea," I said. "Except we don't have a tree house."

"You most certainly do," Nossyss answered. A beam of bright, sparkling light blasted out of his amulet, hit an oak tree, and just like that, a rickety old tree house appeared up at the top, with an old rope ladder hanging down the side.

"Like my father's not gonna notice that thing up there and wonder where it came from?" I said.

"It was here," Imagos said, smiling, "when you bought the house. It's always been there. Isn't that right, Uncle?"

"Exactly," Nossyss agreed.

"You mean you're gonna mess with his mind again?" I asked.

"Just a little, dear," Prognostica said.

"Okay," I said, "but let's not make a habit of it, okay?" The idea of fooling my father like this—even for a good cause—made me feel *incredibly* guilty. "It seems pretty small," I said, looking up at the tree house. "How're you all gonna fit in there?"

With a wave of his trunk, Uncle Nossyss led us all toward the ladder. "Just follow me."

"You guys go ahead," I said. "I don't really like heights. The one time I ever tried to climb the ropes in gym, I freaked out halfway up and got stuck there for half an hour."

Prince Imagos took me by the arm and walked me over to the ladder. "You go up ahead of me, Mehera," he said. "I'll make sure you don't fall."

"Thanks, Your Majesty," I answered. Of course what I *wanted* to say was, "You are absolutely the *hottest* guy I've ever seen in my entire life, and I'd follow you to the *moon* if you asked me to," but luckily I was able to keep my big fat mouth shut.

And up the ladder I went.

My brains nearly melted when I walked through the door. I'd expected to see, well, a *tree house*, but what I walked into was more like a palace. The place stretched on forever, one giant room after another, the walls and ceilings rising up so high I couldn't see where they ended. There were colorful Persian rugs (well, I guess they were *Imaginalian* rugs) and beds with silk curtains and gigantic chandeliers with little mindfires flying around inside them. Best of all, there was table after table heaped, just *heaped*, with the most delicious-looking Imaginalian treats. Once, when Papa'd taken me down to New York City to see a play—*Wicked*, my all-time favorite—we stayed in this super-deluxe fancy hotel. (We couldn't really afford it, but it was my birthday and Papa pretty much does anything I want on my birthday.) Well, let me tell you, that hotel was a *total dump* compared to the tree house. "How did you *do* this?" I asked.

"A fairly complex enchantment," Uncle Nossyss answered, "and, honestly, I'm not certain how long it will last. But, for now, at least—"

"It won't have to last long," Prince Imagos said, "because we won't *be* here long."

"What?" I said. "Why?"

"We're here for one reason and one reason alone," Imagos answered. "To find a way to save the Imaginalians trapped in Nolandia and resurrect our kingdom. And we don't have the luxury of time."

"Which means," Prognostica said, "that the first order of business is to find the Dreamer."

"Mrs. Morice-Gilland?" I asked. "Why?"

"Her belief in us," Prognostica answered, "is even greater than yours." I didn't like hearing that, even though I knew it was probably true. "If you alone could create the Unbelievable Bridge and pluck us out of Nolandia, think what miracles the two of you could manifest together." Making miracles side by side with Mikela Morice-Gilland? Now that was an idea I could get behind.

"But," I asked, "didn't you say that you already tried and you couldn't find her?"

"That," Prognostica said, nibbling on a glowing vegetable that was wrapped up in rainbow-colored leaves, "was when we were in Nolandia. But now that we're here, on the Dreamer's own world, you can rest assured that we *will* find her."

"Tomorrow," Imagos said, yawning, "our efforts begin. For now, we rest."

I said good night and headed for the door—then stopped. I had a terrific idea, but I wasn't sure how it would go over with the Prince.

"Something else, Mehera?" Imagos asked.

"Well, I was wondering . . . and feel free to say no, Your Majesty . . . but I thought, y'know, my dad wouldn't mind if I had *one* friend sleep over tonight, and . . ." I looked over at the Nebulous Seer, then back at the Prince. "Y'think Prognostica could—?"

Imagos sat there for a minute, rubbing his chin and pondering like he was King Solomon and I'd just asked him the most important question in the History of Questions, and then nodded. "But," he warned Prognostica, "be back here first thing in the morning."

Prognostica bowed. "Thank you, my Prince," she said, and I bowed, too. Then—I'm not sure why—we both started giggling like a couple of eight-year-olds and ran out of the room.

It took me twenty minutes to climb down that stupid rope ladder, and I was scared half to death, but the truth is, with Prognostica there I really didn't mind.

CHAPTER SIXTEEN
Visions

My father had no problem with Claire Voyante staying over, so the two of us watched a DVD—the Nebulous Seer had never seen a movie, and I thought she'd love *The Princess Bride* (which she did)—and then Papa ordered us up to bed.

I plopped down on a foam mat on the floor and gave "Claire" my bed. "Y'know what's so weird about all this?" I said as we sat there in the dark.

"What?" Prognostica asked.

"Well, *everything*," I laughed, shooing away this annoying gnat that almost flew up my nose. "But what's really weird is how *not* weird this is. I mean, I just created a magical bridge out of my own thoughts, traveled into another dimension, and brought my favorite fictional characters home with me. I should be having a total nervous breakdown. But it all seems so . . . I dunno . . . *normal* to me. Y'know, in a totally *abnormal* kinda way."

"First of all, Mehera," the Nebulous Seer said, "we're not fictional characters. Never forget that. We're every bit as real as you are."

"Oh, I know," I said. "I didn't mean—"

"I know you didn't." She reached out and patted my hand. "In this world," Prognostica went on, "we're just a story. But, really, the *whole universe* is just a story, isn't it? *Every life* is an extraordinary adventure. Some lives just end up between the pages of a book."

"'Life itself,'" I said, quoting the banner in Papa's store, "'is the most wonderful fairy tale.'"

"Exactly," Prognostica agreed.

We just stretched out there in the dark for a while, in this super-cozy silence (well, silent except for that gnat, which kept buzzing around our heads), and then I asked Prognostica about her visions. "Can you see what's going to happen here? Will I be able to help you all get home again?"

"A very good question, dear," Prognostica said. "Let's find out." The Nebulous Seer sat up in bed, leaned her back against the wall, and began humming. It was a strange tune . . . kind of sweet and kind of creepy at the same time. Her arms started moving, making all these snakelike motions along with the song, and her fingers began twitching like spiders. Then, all of a sudden, the humming stopped, her arms fell limp, and her head slumped forward.

I was all ready to jump onto the bed and begin CPR (not that I knew how) when Prognostica cleared her throat and said, "*Well*, then . . ."

"You okay?" I asked. There was movement under all that hair that *seemed* like she was nodding her head. "And did you . . . y'know . . . have one of your visions?"

"Yes," the Nebulous Seer answered. The tone of her voice had changed, like she'd gone from a flute to an oboe. "I saw a restored Imaginalis, with our young Prince—now wearing the Rajah's crown—sitting upon the throne. I saw the Golden Age predicted by Rajah Merogji. The same Golden Age you glimpsed when you crossed the Bridge, an age of peace and plenty that transcends even the days of the Silver Queen." She paused. Scratched her head. Sighed. "Or maybe not," she said, high and fluty again.

In the stories, Prognostica could never say for sure whether her predictions were going to come true, and those three words—"or maybe not"—always seemed hilarious to me. But this wasn't a book anymore: The entire future of Imaginalis was at stake, and "or maybe not" didn't seem funny to me at all.

Prognostica could tell how worried I was. "You're wondering why I can't be more . . . definitive in my predictions," she said.

"Maybe a little," I whispered. I didn't want to make her feel bad or anything.

The seer leaned over the edge of the bed, her hair falling forward, some of it covering me like a blanket (I couldn't help myself; I ran my fingers through it the same way I'd run them over my furry blanket when I was little). "Understand, dear," Prognostica said, "that there's more than one future. Every choice we make, every action we take, has an impact on how our fates play out. Just now, I saw the future I described. But I also saw *another*, where—" Now her voice went down deep, like a cello. "Well, let's just say that it's not a happy ending."

"Then how," I said, moving closer to Prognostica, "do you know which vision to choose?"

"In the beginning, when my second sight first came to me, I presumed the wisest path was to choose the darkest vision."

"What? Why would you do that?"

"There are times when the surest way to *prevent* a

negative future is to *predict* one."

"You mean," I asked, "that people get so scared by the vision that they do everything they can to stop it?"

"Exactly," Prognostica said. "But I soon realized that fear . . . fear is a dangerous force to play with. Which is why," she went on, "I prefer to simply *choose the vision I like best*. Choosing, sweet Mehera: That's the most magnificent magic of all. Choose the future you want, and you're halfway to manifesting it. As you saw with the Unbelievable Bridge, our belief can be powerful indeed."

"The Bridge," I said. "Something's been bothering me about that."

"Why," Prognostica said, like she was reading my mind (and she probably was), "did we need *you* to create it?"

"Yes," I said. That annoying gnat was back again, dive-bombing us. I tried to catch it between my hands (I hate to kill bugs; whenever I can, I catch them and carry them outside—my mom was the same way), but it was so small I missed. "I mean, Uncle Nossyss—he can stuff a palace into a tree house. And Pralaya, he's one of the greatest sorcerers in the history of Imaginalis. Why did you need *me?*"

Prognostica settled back in the bed. "The Unbelievable Bridge," she said, "is unique. Since time's beginningless beginning, the only one who's ever been able to conjure it was the Silver Queen."

"Then what made you think I could do it?"

"Because you did it before—in your stories."

"You know about my stories?" I asked. I didn't mind it, either. If there was anyone in the whole universe I'd want to share those stories with, it was Prognostica.

"Of course. I saw them, in my visions. That's how we found out about you."

"But they were only *stories*. I made them up, I—"

"The whole universe is just a story," Prognostica said again, "and the line between imagination and reality is a thin one. And for someone like you, Mehera, who has the Silver Queen's spark? Well, we hoped that what you dreamed on paper could manifest in reality. And, by the Rajah's grace, we were right. And we're very grateful to you, Mehera. Very grateful indeed."

I didn't have much time to appreciate what she'd said, because this Hugely Horrible Thought suddenly popped into my head. "Wait, wait, wait," I said. "If *you* knew about my stories, then does that mean Prince Imagos—"

"Has heard about your dream of winning his heart? Becoming his Queen?"

"They weren't *really* my dreams," I said, glad that Prognostica couldn't see me blushing in the dark. "I mean, they were, kinda, but I didn't even know he was *real* then, it was just—"

"Don't worry," Prognostica said. "I didn't share *every* detail of my visions,"

"Swear?" I asked.

"Swear."

"Not that it really matters," I mumbled, adjusting my covers. All of a sudden I was exhausted. "Much."

"Good night, dear," Prognostica whispered.

"G'night, Prognostica," I answered. I ran my fingers through that blanket of golden hair and slipped off into a totally delicious sleep.

CHAPTER SEVENTEEN
Finding the Dreamer

"So," Celeste asked me the following Sunday morning at Queenstown Family, "what's with Porky Boy and Bizarro Girl?" I kept trying to duck her, but she finally cornered me in the pantry. Considering she was stuffing her face with a custard doughnut—*and* I'd been seeing her on the bus in the afternoons—I figured she was definitely over her health kick.

"*Excuse* me?" I said.

"I mean, you dump me and start hanging around some fat kid with a nose the size of a football and some goofy girl in an ugly yellow dress?" She was right, I pretty much *had* dumped her. "The same dress every day," Celeste went on. "What's up with that? And that hair? With those pigtails sticking straight out and those bangs in her eyes, she looks like a sheepdog that stuck its paw in an electrical socket."

That was pretty harsh, but I wondered if Celeste was acting that way because . . . maybe . . . she missed me. I mean, I *was* her best friend. Once. In fact, I was starting to feel so guilty about it that I was kinda sorta considering telling her everything that was going on. "They're nice kids," I said.

"Well, they *totally* creep me out," Celeste said. "They always have. Y'know, I can't figure why you've gone all gaga over these idiots all of a sudden. I mean, you've known them since the first grade." Of course I hadn't, but since Uncle Nossyss and Prognostica—or Ellison and Claire—had been going to school with me every day, we needed some way to explain them, so . . . you guessed it . . . the old elephant put a whammy on the whole school to make people think that they'd always been there. "And what's with that other kid I see you with sometimes? The one who looks like he's *foreign* or something?" She was talking about Imagos. He'd taken some walks around the neighborhood with me. Called them "sociological expeditions," a way to understand our world and its customs. "What's a boy that hot doing hanging out with *you*?"

I couldn't believe she said that to me. I almost said something super awful back—and maybe I would have, if we weren't in a place where we were supposed to be nice to people. Instead I just walked away from her and sat down at one of the tables. I looked over at Celeste— really quick—and she had this weird look on her face, like maybe she felt bad about what she'd said.

"I heard what Fish Face said to you." I hadn't realized that there was a boy already sitting there. He was about fourteen. Tall and skinny, with red hair down to his shoulders and an expression on his face like he thought he was really cool or something. He was wearing a faded old jean jacket, a black T-shirt, and pants so low and baggy I thought they might slide off.

"What'd you say?" I asked.

"Fish Face," he said, nodding his head toward where Celeste was standing in the back. He squinted at me. "You two used t' be friends, right?"

I wanted to say "Who *are* you and why is this any of your business and don't you dare call her Fish Face," but what came out of my mouth was "Friends? Not really." I bit off the end of a fingernail. "Not for a long time, anyway." I folded my arms across my chest. Rolled my eyes. "She's a loser."

"You bet she is," the boy said, getting up and heading for the door. "See ya around." It wasn't until he was walking away that I got a good whiff of him. He smelled awful.

* * *

130

Uncle Nossyss and Prognostica had been going to school with me because Prince Imagos had ordered them to. He said he wanted them to protect me. "As the builder of the Unbelievable Bridge, you are our doorway back to Nolandia and then on to a reborn Imaginalis. If anything happens to you, Mehera, we'll be trapped. Stranded here on your world forever."

"What could possibly happen to me?" I asked the Prince, one afternoon in the tree house. I'd nearly broken my neck climbing up there because this really beautiful butterfly flew by and I was so busy looking at it that I almost fell off the ladder.

"You said yourself," the Prince answered, "that yours is a dangerous world, filled with war, disease, chaos, and tragedy of every kind."

"Indeed," Prognostica said. The main room was filled with computers and televisions that Uncle Nossyss had conjured up. News channels were playing all the time. Websites scrolled across the monitors so fast I could hardly see them. "Your entire planet is an ongoing disaster. Every day, it seems, there's another catastrophe. So much fear and uncertainty and tragedy. However do you bear it?"

"When a pickpocket," Nossyss said, sighing, "looks at a king, he sees only his pockets."

"And what is *that* supposed to mean, m'lord?" Prognostica asked.

"Aren't you the one who says that choosing is the most magnificent magic of all? Well, why are you choosing only to see the darkness in this world?" He didn't give her the chance to answer. "I, too, have been studying Mehera's kingdom"—I loved it when he called it that—"and there is extraordinary beauty here. Light and love, with the potential to build a world every bit as wonderful as Imaginalis."

"You're right, of course." She looked over at the televisions and computers. "But you must admit that this is a strange and terrifying place."

"Look," I told her, "a lot of weird, scary stuff does happen, but, y'know, that's not Queenstown. None of those things ever happen here." At least I didn't *think* they did.

After that, we had another long talk about Mrs. Morice-Gilland. Uncle Nossyss said he was pretty sure that, if we worked together, the Dreamer and I could "unleash a wave of belief powerful enough to restore our lost world." I told them how I'd tried to get in touch with the World's Greatest Writer, and how I'd pretty much failed, but Prince Imagos thought Nossyss's enchantments could do what all my goofy letters and phone calls couldn't.

Every night the old elephant would go into deep meditation, sending out a web of magic searching for Mrs.

Morice-Gilland. But not one of the tracking enchant-ments he zapped across the planet could find her. Every soul mirror he looked into didn't show him anything but his own face staring back. Prognostica, meanwhile, kept looking into the future—all futures, *any* future, and even a few pasts—for even a quick glimpse of the Dreamer, but she never found a thing. "Do you think," I asked, kind of sick and scared by the thought, "that Mrs. Morice-Gilland could be, y'know . . ." I didn't want to say it, but I had to. "Dead?"

"No," Uncle Nossyss answered. "If that were the case, I would know it. This is very different. She's hidden herself behind a spell of concealment."

"Wait, wait," I said, "she's hidden *herself*? Are you telling me that Mrs. Morice-Gilland is some kind of sor-ceress?"

"Not in the way you're imagining it," Nossyss said. "People don't necessarily need to know magic to weave a spell. In fact, I'd guess that many in your kingdom are doing magic all the time, without even realizing it."

"How?" I asked.

"All it takes," Nossyss said, "is intention. And will. And not necessarily *conscious* will. If Mrs. Morice-Gilland is one of those people who want nothing more in life than to be left alone—"

"I'm pretty sure that she is," I said.

"Well, then," Nossyss went on, "when a person lives that way, year after year after year, blocking out the world, keeping other people at a distance, it engages a deep and powerful *personal* magic. Eventually an actual barrier of energy will rise up around her. To all intents and purposes, she will become invisible."

Prince Imagos leaned forward. "So you're saying that you won't be able to find the Dreamer?"

"No, my Prince," Nossyss replied. "I'm saying that it will take more time."

"We don't *have* more time!" Imagos shouted. I'd never heard him raise his voice before, never seen him angry. It didn't frighten me—I could never be scared of Imagos—it just made me want to do something, *anything*, to help him. "The longer we remain here, the more likely it is that, when we return to Nolandia, our people will be . . ." His voice trailed off.

Nossyss bowed his head. His ears drooped. "I will double my efforts, Your Highness," he said.

And that's when I had a fantastic idea. "Maybe," I said, "you won't have to."

"What are you talking about, Mehera?" Prognostica asked.

"Nancy Drew," I said.

CHAPTER EIGHTEEN
The Agent

I was shrieking at the top of my lungs. It was Saturday night, and me and Prognostica (Prognostica and I?) were in an astral tunnel—kind of like a water slide made out of light—skidding across something Uncle Nossyss called the Etheria, so fast I thought was going to end up *ahead* of myself. I *should* have been terrified, but no kidding, it was more fun than I'd ever had in my entire life. All around me, the tunnel was whirling and sparking and crackling. I could actually see through the walls, getting glimpses of . . . well, of *the entire world*. It was like everyone on Earth, every*where* on Earth, was whipping past me (or was I whipping past it?) at a speed so amazing that it should have all been a blur. But it wasn't. (Guess that's why they call it magic.) Uncle Nossyss had explained that we'd be stepping out of the Gross

World—"the world of forms," he explained—and into the Etheria, "the world of energy," using the tunnel as a shortcut to our destination. Honestly, I hadn't understood a word of it, and considering the fun I was having, I really didn't care.

"Are you all right, dear?" Prognostica asked, sliding along next to me, her hair whipping out in every direction.

"You kidding?" I whooped. I saw a flock of geese fly by, followed by an Egyptian pyramid, a football team, the space shuttle, an old lady in a nursing home, the entire city of Rome, Italy, and a family of polar bears. "This is fantastic!" I hooted. "This is incredible!" Papa thought I was sleeping over at Claire's house—in fact, he'd even spoken to Claire's mother on the phone (one more enchantment for me to feel guilty about). If he could have seen what I was really doing, he probably would have been on the phone with the FBI, the CIA , the FAA, and Auntie Pat.

An hour before that, we'd been in my kitchen. Papa was working late at the store, and I was sitting around the table with the Companions, eating an Imaginalian dessert called walloom (it's made out of custard, chocolate, stardust, and moonbeams. Believe me, if you've never eaten a moonbeam, you don't know what you're missing). I pretty much convinced the others that the best way to find Mrs. Morice-Gilland was good old-fashioned detective work. Well, good old-fashioned *illegal* detective work: I told them that we needed to go down to Manhattan and break into the office of Morice-Gilland's agent, Gerald Epstein. "I can't believe," I told them, "that I didn't think of this in the first place. I mean, he's gotta have her address there somewhere. How hard could it be to find it?"

The Prince and Nossyss weren't so sure this was a good idea. "Aside from being illegal," Imagos said, "it's also immoral." But Prognostica agreed with me that, since we *had* to find Mrs. Morice-Gilland in order to save everyone in Imaginalis, just a *little* breaking and entering wouldn't hurt.

"Besides," I said, "it's not like we're actually stealing anything. We're just getting the address and going on our way. It's no different," I said, turning to Uncle Nossyss, "than you using one of your spells to find her."

"I suppose," Nossyss said—but I could tell he wasn't totally convinced. Still, he agreed to whip up an astral tunnel and travel with Prognostica the hundred miles to New York City. He said that if he did the spell right, it would take only a few minutes to get there.

"Oh, no," I said, "that's *my* world out there, my

kingdom. I know it better than any of you. I should go with Prognostica." I licked some walloom off my spoon and smiled. "Besides, when am I ever gonna get another chance to ride in an astral tunnel?"

Nossyss and the Prince looked at each other—it was like they were talking without saying anything—and then the Prince nodded. "The tunnel will get them in and out quickly. I don't see the harm. But," he said to Nossyss, "you keep a mirror open and watch them carefully. At the first sign of trouble, pull them back."

"Of course, my Prince," the old elephant answered. "But what if I *can't* pull them back in time? What if they're captured by the authorities? Locked away in a dungeon for a thousand years?"

I grinned. "Well, then I guess you'll just have to come and rescue us."

The old elephant thought about that, smiled, and said, "Sounds like fun." But I could tell he was still worried.

We landed, a little too fast and a little too hard, on the floor. The tunnel was gone for now, and we were standing in a dark office: small, cramped, and stuffy. I didn't dare turn on the lights, but as best I could see, there were two desks, one computer—a Mac that must have been like twenty years old—some file cabinets, a big old couch covered in blankets, a few of those uncomfortable metal office chairs, and stacks and stacks of books. There were a bunch of framed photos hanging on the walls, and all of them showed the same hugely fat, curly-haired guy standing with people who I *guess* were famous (they sure *posed* like they were, but honestly, I didn't recognize a single one). The whole place looked like it hadn't been dusted since before my parents were born. "What a dump," I whispered. "This Epstein guy can't be much of an agent. Which, considering what a great job he did with the Imaginalis books, makes a lot of sense."

"Mrs. Morice-Gilland," Prognostica said, "is trying to keep herself concealed. A representative like this would certainly help her do that."

"That's for sure," I said, heading for one of the desks. "Wish we had a flashlight."

Prognostica touched her own forehead with her pointer finger, kind of drew a small circle there, then tapped three times. A tiny, glowing mindfire, the size of a soap bubble, popped out of her head, drifting around the room for a while, then settling down next to me. "Will this do, dear?" the Nebulous Seer asked.

I smiled, nodded, and then sat down at the first desk, looking through each of the drawers. "How, exactly, do those things work?" I asked.

"Our minds," Prognostica explained, looking through the other desk, "are filled with random thoughts we don't need, thoughts we'll never use, even if we live forever. Millions and millions of them, flitting around with no purpose. I'm sure you've noticed them."

"Yeah," I said to the seer, "sometimes there's so much junk in my head, I have no clue where it came from." I turned on the computer. The sound, when it booted up, was a little too loud (well, it seemed that way to me), and I looked over at the door, expecting a dozen policemen to come busting in and arrest us. "It's like I'm not even thinking it."

"In a way," Prognostica answered, "you're not. The mind, well, it has a mind of its own. When we're not using it, it just keeps . . . thinking away. And most of those thoughts are what I call brain junk. When we create mindfires, we're taking the energy of that brain junk and converting it to light." When Prognostica said it, it sounded so easy, but I knew I could never do that. "Maybe one day you could teach me how to—" I looked at the computer screen and groaned.

"What?" Prognostica asked.

"You need a password to get in."

"What's a password?" Prognostica asked. When

I explained, the Nebulous Seer just laughed, rolled her chair over next to me, leaned in toward the computer screen, and started humming to it. It was a pretty song, and she did a great job humming it, but I couldn't understand what the *point* was.

Then the computer screen flashed and the desktop appeared.

"How did you do that?" I asked.

"Music," Prognostica said, "is the oldest language in creation. And every creature in every universe understands it, if you know the right notes to sing."

"Are you saying that you used music to ask the computer to let you in?"

"Absolutely, dear."

"I guess," I said, shrugging, "that's no weirder than sliding across the Etheria. Can you ask it to find Mrs. Morice-Gilland's address for us?"

The Nebulous Seer hummed again and . . . okay, you're not going to believe this, but it's true . . . the computer *hummed back*, a bunch of electronic beeps and boops that made a song kinda sorta like Prognostica's. "What'd it say?" I asked.

"Roughly translated," Prognostica answered, "it said, 'Find it yourself.'"

I stuck my tongue out at the computer. "Don't have to

be rude about it," I said. I started looking through Gerald Epstein's files, his digital address book, every desktop folder, but I couldn't find *anything* about the Imaginalis books or Mrs. Morice-Gilland anywhere. "It's got to be here. He's her *agent*, he's supposed to—"

That's when I heard this weird snorting sound behind us, like some wild animal getting ready to attack. Prognostica and I both whirled around to see a figure stretched out on the couch, moving around under the blankets, changing positions, grunting, and gurgling, then finally sighing and settling back down to sleep.

"Oh, no," I whispered. "He must've been there all along, and we didn't even see him." I looked at the guy on the couch, then over at the photos on the wall. Couch Man was older, his hair was all gray now—but it was Gerald Epstein, for sure. "This is terrible."

"This," Prognistica said, "is *wonderful.*" The seer moved quickly, some of her hair shooting out like an octopus tentacle and wrapping around Epstein—lifting him up off the couch and dropping him down in an office chair. Epstein's eyes flew open, and he started to let out this major scream when another hair tentacle wrapped around his mouth and pretty much shut him up.

"What are you *doing?*" I asked, totally panicked.

"We could be here all night and never find that

address," Prognostica said, totally calm. "But *he knows*, dear."

I wasn't the only one having a panic attack. Gerald Epstein's eyes looked like they were going to explode out of his head. "You're scaring him," I said to Prognostica. "What if he has a heart attack or something?"

"Heart attack?" Prognostica asked. "Is that bad?"

"Very," I said.

Prognostica leaned in toward Epstein. "If I release you, dear," she asked him, "do you promise not to scream?" He nodded, and she let him go.

Epstein didn't make a sound, just sat there and stared at Prognostica—which seems like the right thing to do when you're face-to-face with a woman whose entire body is covered in hair. "Mr. Epstein," I said, "we didn't mean to frighten you, we didn't even think you'd *be* here—"

"I—I sleep here sometimes," he croaked. I leaned in closer to hear him and noticed that he reeked of cologne.

"Why?" I asked.

Epstein shrugged. "My wife threw me out of the house a few months ago, and y'know, it's cheaper than a hotel and . . ." He got this super-deluxe annoyed look on his face. "And why am I telling you this? Who *are* you?" He looked over at Prognostica. "And *what* are you?"

"You'd never believe it," I said. "Look, we really don't wanna bother you, and we're *really* sorry we broke in to your office—"

"Broke in?" Epstein said. He looked around—to see if we'd damaged anything, I guess—and noticed that the door was still locked. From the inside. "How did you—?"

"You wouldn't believe that, either. Anyway, like I said, we'll leave right now, but we need you to tell us where she lives."

"She?" Epstein asked.

"Mikela Morice-Gilland," I answered. "We have to find her right away."

From the expression on his face, you'd think I had asked him to help us find the Easter Bunny. "Mikela Morice-Gilland?" he said. He looked over at Prognostica again, and all of a sudden he started laughing. "Oh, my *God*," he said. "That's a *costume*! You're fans! You're Imaginalis fans!"

"Isn't everyone?" Prognostica asked.

Epstein couldn't stop laughing. "And you," he said, turning back to me, "I'll just bet you're that crazy kid who wrote that four-hundred-page letter."

"Maybe," I said, embarrassed. "It's not very nice, y'know, calling me crazy."

"I'm sorry, I'm sorry," Epstein said. "I didn't mean

it that way. It's just . . . you have to understand. You're the only Imaginalis fan who ever wrote to me in all the years those books were coming out. The only one." He ran a hand through his hair, playing with his curls, then looked over at me with this really sad smile. "I wanted to help you out, I really did. But I had an agreement with Morice-Gilland and—" He noticed the mindfire, floating around above our heads. "What *is* that?"

I ignored the question. "Where does she live, Mr. Epstein?" I asked.

"I can't tell you," Epstein said. "And believe me, it's better for you. The last person you'd ever want to meet is Mikela Morice-Gilland."

"What?" I asked. "Why?"

"You just don't," he said. "Anyway, we have an agreement. A contract." He looked at both of us and smiled again. "It's sweet, actually, that the two of you care so much that you'd pull a nutty stunt like this. I'd like to tell you where to find her, really. I mean, I'd go with you, just to see her face . . . but a deal's a deal."

"Fine," I said, angry now, turning back to the computer. "I'll find it myself."

"It's not in there, kiddo," Epstein said. "Old bat wouldn't let me write any of her personal stuff down anywhere."

"Don't call her that," I said. "She is not an old—"

"Mr. Epstein," Prognostica interrupted, her voice sounding like a flute and a violin playing together, "you must keep the information somewhere."

Epstein smiled—Prognotisca's voice seemed to be relaxing him—and tapped his head. "In here. Photographic memory. Been that way since I was a kid. Facts, figures, names, addresses, all stored away upstairs." He pointed to the Mac. "And unlike that old dinosaur, *this* baby hasn't crashed yet."

"Really, dear?" Prognostica said. "That's *so* interesting." She closed her eyes, concentrated for a moment—and then the mindfire flew *straight into Gerald Epstein's mouth*. He squawked like a rooster, then his whole body totally stiffened while the mindfire moved up, into his head—I could actually see its light flickering behind his eyes—and, finally, out his left ear.

"Wh-what did you do?" Epstein said.

"Don't worry, dear, you'll be just fine," Prognostica said as the mindfire landed in her open palm. She held it against her forehead, humming to it. Then she turned to me: "Twelve Walnut Road, Black Mountain, North Carolina."

"Wait a minute, wait a minute," I said, "How did you—?"

"Takes a thought to find a thought," Prognostica said.

Epstein stared at the sparkling little light, his mouth hanging open. "That's—that's a mindfire," he said. "Like in Mikela's books." He turned back to Prognostica, studying her like she was some kind of science experiment, then suddenly jumped forward and yanked at her hair—"Hey! Stop that!" I yelled—tossing back layer after layer after layer. But for every layer he got through, he found ten more underneath it. The hair pretty much went on forever.

"Impossible," Epstein muttered.

"I agree," said Prognostica.

"I must be dreaming," he said.

"That I'm not so sure about, dear."

And then the astral tunnel exploded into the room. Prognostica took my hand, and we jumped in.

Gerald Epstein jumped in after us.

CHAPTER NINETEEN
Transparent

"What are you *doing* here?" I shouted when I saw Gerald Epstein dropping out of the tunnel behind us, falling flat on his butt. "Why did you follow us? Are you crazy?"

Epstein looked like he might *be* crazy. His eyes were bugging out as he looked around the palace, down at himself, then over at me and Prognostica. He tried to say something, but all that came out were these caveman grunts and mumbles. Then he finally cleared his throat and said, "Wh-where am I? Is this—is this Imaginalis?"

"Don't be silly," I said. "You're in a tree house in Queenstown, New York."

"Tree house," Epstein said. A group of mindfires flew over his head. "Queenstown. Right."

Prognostica got to her feet, then helped Epstein up.

(And, believe me, it wasn't easy. That guy must have weighed three hundred pounds.) "I don't understand," Prognostica said. "I was sure I sealed the tunnel behind us—"

"But you clearly didn't," someone said. We turned to see Prince Imagos standing there. And he didn't look happy.

"Oh, my God, it *is* true!" Gerald Epstein said, rushing over to the Prince, poking at him to see if he was real. (It was an *incredibly* rude thing to do, especially to a prince, but, all things considered, I kind of understood.) "Prince Imagos!" he shouted. "Holy moley, it's Prince Imagos!" He looked over at me. "You've gotta understand. From the time I read the first manuscript for the first Imaginalis book, I had this . . . feeling. It was like I wasn't reading a work of fiction at all. Like I was reading a story that had really happened, in a world that actually existed. I never told anyone . . . well, once I mentioned it to Trish, that's my wife, soon-to-be *ex*-wife . . . and the woman gave me *such* a look. Anyway, I think that's why I put up with Morice-Gilland and all her nutty demands for so many years. Because, somewhere, deep down, I—I always believed." For a second he looked like he was going to cry. "*I always believed,*" he repeated. "And I guess that's why I jumped into the tunnel after you."

Prince Imagos just sort of glared at Mr. Epstein (now he was the one being rude, and I couldn't understand why), raised his hand, and waved it over that curly gray head. "And now it's time to *unbelieve*," the Prince said. I didn't know what was wrong, but he sure didn't sound like himself. "I may not be the sorcerer that Lord Nossyss is, but I do have the ability to wipe your mind clean, send you back where you came from, and—"

"No! No, you can't!" I said, racing over to them. "It's bad enough what you've all done, what I *let* you do, to my father, but you can't solve every problem by messing with people's minds like this. It's not right. Besides," I went on, "if Mr. Epstein believes, then maybe *he* has the Silver Queen's spark, too, and he might be able to help us to—"

"How dare you," Prince Imagos roared, "question my actions?" His eyes got so wild that I flinched and threw my arm across my face. For a second there, just for a second, I had this crazy thought that maybe he was going to hit me or something.

He didn't, of course. He never would. In fact, when I looked up at him, I couldn't believe it. There were *tears* in his eyes. "Oh, Mehera," he said, "I'm so sorry. I shouldn't have shouted. It isn't you." He looked over at Epstein. "It isn't even *him*. I just . . ."

Prognostica rushed to the Prince's side. "What's wrong, Your Highness?" She put out a hand, moved her fingers like she was reading invisible energies in the air. Which I guess she was. "Oh, no." She made a sound like a broken flute. "Lord Nossyss!"

The old elephant was shivering underneath his blankets, staring up at us but not really seeing. Prognostica wiped the sweat off his forehead with the ends of her hair.

"It happened suddenly," Imagos said, "not long after you left. Uncle said he felt dizzy, weak, and he just . . . collapsed."

"What is it?" I asked. "Some kinda flu or something?"

The Nebulous Seer's whole body shook then, like she'd suddenly been caught in an earthquake from the inside out. "No, dear," she said, and I could tell that she was struggling not to cry. "I should have seen this. At least the *possibility* of it."

"We have all," the Prince said gently, "had other things on our minds, Prognostica. Don't blame yourself."

"Seen what?" I asked. "I don't understand."

"Look at him closely, Mehera," Imagos said.

I looked down at Uncle's face—and gasped. Patches

of his skin had become clear and a little shiny, kind of like plastic wrap. I could actually see through him, to the pillows underneath his head. "How—?"

"*You* may have the spark of Imaginalis in you, dear," Prognostica said. "But *we* don't have the spark of Earth. There is only one world in all the universes that we were made for, that we belong in. And with Imaginalis lost to us—"

"All of us," Prince Imagos said, finishing her thought, "will eventually be pulled back into Nolandia. And then—"

"No," Uncle Nossyss said, reaching his trunk out and wrapping it around my hand. "No, it will not happen that way. Because Mehera will find the Dreamer . . . and together they will save us all."

"No. No, this isn't right." I turned and pointed to the Prince. "He's the hero of the story." And then back at Nossyss. "And you . . . you're the one who always helps him save the day. You figure out the clues, make the plans. Everyone's depending on you. You can't just—"

"Perhaps," Imagos replied, "this isn't *our* story anymore, Mehera. Perhaps it's *yours*."

"Don't *say* that. I'm just a . . . a supporting character. I'm not important. We need *you*, Uncle Nossyss." I felt totally weird all of a sudden, dizzy and scared and sick to my stomach. It felt like there was something inside me, something old and dark and scary (I can't explain it any better than that) that was trying to fight its way out. "Oh, please, you can't die. You just *can't*."

Uncle Nossyss smiled at me, and it was like he put all his magic in it, like that one small smile sent all his faith, his trust, his belief shooting right into me. "I have no intention of dying," he said. The old elephant closed his eyes, sighed. "Find the Dreamer, Mehera," he said, drifting off.

We all stood there—not saying a word, super-deluxe worried—till Prognostica started humming. I turned to see that she was caught up in another vision, arms moving, fingers twitching. A minute or so later, she stopped humming and said, "We have two days, perhaps three, to find the Dreamer." Her voice sounded shaky now, like someone playing a flute for the first time. "And then it will be too late for him. Too late for *all* of us."

"Wait," I said. "I thought you always have more than one vision . . . and then you choose the better one. The hopeful vision."

"This *is* the hopeful vision," Prognostica answered.

"But—but aren't you even gonna say 'or maybe not'?"

"Not this time." Prognostica sighed.

"It's time to go," the Prince said.

"Yes," Prognostica agreed. "We should go immediately, before—"

"No, Prognostica," Imagos said. "You stay by Uncle's side. He needs you."

Prognostica nodded. "I will serve my lord Nossyss," she said, "till the very end."

"Let's hope it doesn't come to that," Imagos said, his body starting to shimmer, his features changing, till he was thirteen-year-old Sonny Royal again. "And now, Mehera," Sonny went on, turning toward me, "let's go find the Dreamer."

"Not without me, you're not." It was Gerald Epstein, who'd been standing in the corner of the room, watching everything.

"*You* can't come," I said.

"You think," Epstein said, and I could see that it took a lot of courage for him to speak up, "you're just gonna show up at her house and she's gonna let you in? Just like that? The old bat hates people."

"And she doesn't hate you?" I asked.

"Well, yeah," Epstein said, "she pretty much *loathes* me. But at least she *knows* me, which means we've got at least a slight chance of actually getting in the door."

"Why bother with the door?" Prognostica asked.

"Tunnel in, grab her, and force her to do what we need her to do!"

"Would you really," Sonny asked, "have us treat the Dreamer in such way?"

The seer bowed her head (at least I think she did). "No, my Prince," she said quietly.

Sonny walked over to Gerald Epstein. "All right," he said, "you can come with us." He sniffed once, twice. Winced. "But with all due respect, Mr. Epstein, could you *please* wash off that cologne?"

CHAPTER TWENTY
Mrs. Morice-Gilland

But there was no time for washing. Another astral tunnel was quickly conjured up, and the three of us jumped in. The trip was a little longer this time—it took close to ten minutes—but pretty soon we found ourselves standing in the hot morning sun at the bottom of a long dirt driveway, an old station wagon parked up at the top facing a tiny cottage that looked like it hadn't been painted since . . . well, *ever*. Looking at the cottage, I had this weird feeling that if I turned away for a second, it might actually disappear. But here's what's even weirder: There were these humongaramous old trees around the house—it was like they were guarding the place—and I could swear that I could hear them (well, *almost* hear them, like their voices were miles under the ground) demanding that the three of us get out of there, right away, or face the consequences. And the consequences wouldn't be very good, either.

"Can you feel it?" Sonny asked. "The barrier she's erected around herself? Her personal magic, trying to drive us away."

"You *sure* she's not some kind of sorceress?" I said as we walked up the driveway. It felt like we were walking through something that was alive . . . and *thick*. Something that could, if it wanted to, kick us all the way back to Queenstown.

"Not sorcery," Sonny said. "Just loneliness."

"Loneliness?" I said. "But that doesn't even make sense. I mean, if she's so lonely, why would she go out of her way to avoid people? To keep them away?"

"You tell me," Sonny answered, and he gave me this really funny look.

"*Me?*" I said. "How would *I* know?"

"How indeed," Sonny said.

By the time we reached the front porch, we were wasted—not from the climb, but from pushing against Mrs. Morice-Gilland's personal magic. Epstein flopped down on the steps, totally out of breath. "I *really* need to lose some weight," he said. "I've been meaning to join a gym, but—"

"You can rest later," I said, yanking him back to his

feet, shoving him toward the door. "Now go ahead."

"Maybe it's not such a good idea," Epstein said. The poor guy looked like a total nervous wreck. "You have no idea what she's like. She—"

I let him have the full squint-glare. It didn't work on him, either. Why, I thought, do I even bother? Epstein took a deep breath, then walked up to the front door and knocked. He waited maybe ten seconds and then said, "Nobody home." He turned and started to leave.

"Again," Sonny said.

"Okay, okay." Epstein sighed. He knocked again, a little louder this time. "Hello?" he called. "Mrs. Morice-Gilland? It's Gerald Epstein. Y'know, your agent? All the way from New York." He knocked again. "Mikela?"

We waited for a minute, two, three. Nothing.

"Obviously she's not here," Epstein said.

I pointed to the station wagon. "Her car's here."

"That rusted-out hunk of junk," Epstein said, "looks like it's been there for thirty years."

"Thirty-four, actually," said a voice that sounded very British and very annoyed.

We turned to see a woman standing there. Her face was smeared with dirt, and she had garden tools in her hands. She was tall—bigger than my dad, and he's almost six feet—with white hair pulled back in a tight bun and a nose like a hawk. She was wearing a dirty old canvas apron over a loose-fitting man's shirt and a baggy pair of beat-up jeans. Wow, I thought, she dresses even worse than I do. She had lines all over her face that looked as deep as the Grand Canyon and these three yucky hairs sticking out from the tip of her chin. But, if you looked at her, *really* looked, you could see that Mikela Morice-Gilland had probably been beautiful once, a long, long time ago. "Who the devil are you?" she asked. "And what are you doing on my front porch?"

"Are you *sure*," I whispered to Sonny, "she's not a witch?"

Sonny didn't answer, just jabbed Gerald Epstein with his elbow. Epstein stood there, his mouth hanging open, his hands shaking. "M-Mrs. Morice-Gilland, it's me," he finally said, taking a couple of steps forward and then a few steps back. "Gerald Epstein."

The old lady stomped up the porch steps, and she was mad. "How do I know you're Gerald Epstein?"

"Wait a minute," I said. "You mean you two have never actually met?"

"We've talked on the phone," Epstein said.

Mrs. Morice-Gilland whirled around and looked down at me. "Who are you?" she asked.

I looked up into that wrinkled old face, those angry

159

old eyes. Whoever this was, she wasn't the Mikela Morice-Gilland I'd been imagining since I was seven. She was more like the Wicked Witch of the West. "Mehera Beatrice Crosby," I croaked. "I'm, ah . . . I'm Mr. Epstein's niece." I pointed to Sonny. "And that's my brother, Sonny Royal."

Mrs. Morice-Gilland looked at me like I was a complete nutsoid. "Your last name is Crosby and your brother's is Royal?"

"Half-brother," I said quickly. "Or is it stepbrother?"

"Don't you know?" Mrs. Morice-Gilland asked.

"I-it's one or the other," I answered. "I'm not really sure."

Morice-Gilland mumbled something under her breath, pushed past us, and opened the front door. "Good-bye," she said—and it was pretty clear from the tone of her voice that she meant it.

Before she could slam the door, Epstein rushed forward, grabbing for his wallet, pulling out his driver's license, his credit cards, trying to prove to Mrs. Morice-Gilland that he was who he said he was. She looked the cards over and nodded. "So?" she said.

"So," Epstein said, "could we just come in for a few minutes? We've been traveling around, spring vacation and all, and the kids, they love your books, just love 'em . . . and I thought, y'know, wouldn't it be great if we could stop by and visit Mrs. Morice-Gilland and—"

"And you didn't even think to call?"

"You don't have a phone anymore," Epstein said. "Ma'am," he added.

Morice-Gilland threw her garden tools to the porch floor, looking me and Sonny over. It was like she had X-ray eyes and could see right through us. "Imaginalis is dead and buried. If you're still reading those books, you're wasting your time. And right now you're wasting mine."

"We're very sorry, Mrs. Morice-Gilland," I piped in. "And we promise we'll leave you alone. But I wonder if my brother could just have a glass of water before we go. I mean, he's got asthma—"

Sonny started coughing, really loud. And really fake. He was a terrific prince but a lousy actor.

"—and we walked all this way up the driveway and it's *so hot*—"

"Walked?" Morice-Gilland said. She looked around. "Where's your car?"

"We . . . we parked it up the road," I said, quickly. "Uncle Gerald was afraid that if you saw us driving up, you'd never answer the door."

"And he was right." Mrs. Morice-Gilland stopped,

looking at us all like we were the three ugliest cockroaches that had ever crawled up out of the North Carolina dirt, and then, letting out a gigantor sigh, said, "All right, come on in, have your water—and go."

"One more, please," Sonny asked, emptying his glass.

"One more?" Mrs. Morice-Gilland asked. She'd taken off the apron, washed the dirt off her face, let her hair down—and she still scared me half to death. "That's your third. How much water can one boy drink?"

"Just one more, please?" Sonny pleaded. We were sitting in the living room, which was pretty cramped and had these old, warped wooden floors. Two old couches. An even older love seat. There was a piano that looked like it was about to collapse and, on top of it, a faded photo of Mrs. Morice-Gilland and her husband on their wedding day. (She really *was* beautiful when she was younger.) There were boxes and boxes of moldy books everywhere. In fact, the entire house smelled moldy. I always get headaches from mold, but it was still better than the nauseating stink of Gerald Epstein's cologne.

"One more," Mrs. Morice-Gilland said, stomping off into the kitchen, "and then on your way."

"When," I said to Sonny, "are you going to tell her who you are?"

"I've been trying to the whole time," Sonny answered, and he looked really worried. "But her personal magic is so powerful that the words keep getting trapped in my mouth. Perhaps Uncle Nossyss could get through to her, but I—"

"You've got to try harder," I said. "You've *got* to, or—"

"Duck and cover," Epstein whispered. "She's back."

"Here," the old woman said, handing Sonny the refilled glass. "Are you sure you two don't want anything before I throw you out?" she went on, turning to me and Mr. Epstein.

"No, thanks," I said.

Epstein's stomach gurgled. "Now that you mention it," he said, "I am a little hungry."

"I wasn't offering you a *meal*, just a drink." She rolled her eyes. (I made a note to myself never to do that to my father again. It was really rude.) "As pathetic a specimen as I'd always imagined," she said. "Worst agent on the planet."

Epstein looked miserable, like he knew she was right. "I'm sure he did his best," I said.

"Don't defend the man," Mrs. Morice-Gilland answered. "He's an absolute disaster."

My "brother" finished his water, and Mrs. Morice-

Gilland practically pushed the three of us toward the front door. "*Do* something," I whispered to Sonny.

"Mrs. Morice-Gilland," Sonny said, stopping at the door and looking up at the old woman. "Could you do me just one small favor before we go?"

"*Now* what?" Mrs. Morice-Gilland asked.

"See me," Sonny said.

"Excuse me?"

"See me," Sonny repeated.

Mrs. Morice-Gilland grabbed Sonny by the collar, shoving him—maybe a little too hard—across the room. "It's been lovely visiting with you," she said.

He pulled away from her, whirled around. "*See me,*" he said again. I could actually feel the Prince's personal magic—all his power, all his authority—pushing against Mrs. Morice-Gilland's. "*Really* see."

From the look on the old woman's face, that's exactly what she was doing. "Prince Imagos!" Mrs. Morice-Gilland yelped—and then she fainted.

CHAPTER TWENTY-ONE
The Creation

The Prince caught Mrs. Morice-Gilland before she hit the floor and carried her over to the couch. I'd never seen anyone faint—*really* faint—before, and it spooked me. The way the color rushed out of the old woman's face, the way her eyes rolled back in her head when she dropped . . . Well, I decided right then and there that my fainting days were over forever.

It didn't take long for Mrs. Morice-Gilland to come around, but when she did, she took another look at Prince Imagos and fainted again. "Maybe this wasn't such a good idea," Gerald Epstein said.

Prince Imagos looked at Epstein, and I could swear he used the squint-glare on him. "She needs to see me as I am," he said. He turned back to the old woman, waving his hand in the air, muttering something in a language that sounded like nothing I'd ever heard before, but, somehow, was more familiar than English. ("A simple revival spell that Uncle taught me," he explained.) Mrs. Morice-Gilland opened her eyes again as soon as he was done. "Don't be afraid," he said to her. "You have no truer friend in all the worlds."

Mrs. M-G just kept staring at him like she still couldn't believe what she was seeing. She reached out to touch his face, then yanked her hand back like she'd just touched a hot burner on the stove. The Prince took her hand in his and moved it across his cheek. (He was so gentle with her, so sweet and tender, that I almost cried just watching him.) "Real," he whispered. "As you've always suspected."

"*How?*" was all Mrs. Morice-Gilland could say.

"Let me tell you," Imagos said. He turned to me, smiled. "Let *us* tell you."

"I can't deny that I'm shocked," Mrs. Morice-Gilland said when we were done with our story. "But at the same time, I'm not the least bit surprised." She was pacing back and forth now, sipping a cup of hot tea. She kept looking at Prince Imagos like he was some brontosaurus skeleton from the Museum of Natural History that had suddenly come to life. "Some part of me has always believed. It was—"

"That's just what *I* said," Gerald Epstein interrupted. "It's like I always knew. From the first time, I—"

Mrs. Morice-Gilland's gave Epstein *a look*—it was kind of like my squint-glare, only it worked—and that's all it took for him to zip it. "Sorry," he mumbled.

"You were saying," Imagos reminded the old woman, "that you always knew?"

This sadness kind of swam up into Mrs. Morice-Gilland's eyes. "Writing those first three books," she said, "was pure magic. You have to understand, before I started work on *The Prince of Imaginalis*, the only fiction I'd ever written was when I was young." She smiled for the first time, and it was amazing how much it changed her face. She kind of looked like the Mrs. Morice-Gilland I'd been imagining all those years. "As a little girl, I'd actually write my own Wonderland stories. Put myself into them in place of Alice."

I was sitting on the floor in the corner, and I almost jumped up and shouted, "That's exactly what *I do* with Imaginalis," but the last thing I was going to do was make that cranky old lady mad again.

"Then, when I was in my twenties," Mrs. Morice-Gilland went on, "I wrote two ever-so-serious novels, filled with endless suffering and existential despair.

Thank heaven no one was stupid enough to publish them. After that, I found a niche for myself, writing books and articles on gardening. Gardening, can you imagine? But they were successful, in their modest way, and they gave me some small pleasure. And some small income." She looked over at the wedding photo on the piano, and I couldn't help thinking of that phrase she'd used in *Flight from Forever*: "trapped between the seconds." That's exactly what those two people in the picture were. Trapped there forever. "But after Edward passed . . . well, I had a difficult time of it. I stopped caring about growing things. What was the point, after all, since eventually they'd just die?" When she said that, I got this sick feeling in the pit of my stomach, although I wasn't sure why.

Mrs. M-G put her tea down on the coffee table and lowered herself down onto the couch. I swear I could hear her bones creaking. "I stopped caring. About everything. I shuffled around this old house like a ghost, haunting myself. And then one day . . ." She smiled again, for just a couple of seconds; then it was gone. "I had nothing better to do, I suppose. I went up in the attic and started digging through years and years of junk. The debris of a lifetime. And I found a photo album. Pictures of me in India, when I was a little girl.

Pictures of my father and mother."

This time I couldn't shut my big mouth. "Just like the album my mother had," I said. "She went to India with my dad, right after college, and they—"

"And why," Mrs. Morice-Gilland snapped, cutting me off, "would I care about that?"

"I—I don't know," I said, feeling like a super-deluxe idiot. "I just thought that—"

"Please go on, Mrs. Morice-Gilland," Prince Imagos said, gently. "This is important."

Mrs. Morice-Gilland shot me the same nasty look she'd given Mr. Epstein—it worked on me, too—then turned to the Prince. For a moment that look of amazement came back, like she just couldn't believe he was sitting there across from her (I could sure relate to that). "I must have spent hours going through them," she went on. "Each photo was like a spark in my mind, setting off a blaze of memories. It was like I'd moved through time. As if I couldn't tell whether it was now or then. If I was six or sixty. So many memories . . . so many stories . . . of that other world. And to me, that's what India was. Not another country, another *world*. Dorothy couldn't have felt more amazed when the tornado dropped her in Oz."

I almost blurted out something about how much I

love the Oz books, but I decided against it. (Hey, I'm not a *total* moron.)

"And suddenly," Morice-Gilland went on, "I thought, Wouldn't it be wonderful to write about it all? A memoir . . . about a lost little girl, plunked down in the midst of the most exotic fairyland of all? I'd found a sandalwood figure of the Hindu elephant god, Ganesha . . . the remover of obstacles, they call him in India . . . up in the attic, and I brought it down to my office for good luck. Blew the dust off my IBM Selectric typewriter and started writing."

"And the stories came?" Imagos asked.

Mrs. Morice-Gilland shook her head. "*Nothing* came. Each day I'd try to write about India, and each day I'd fail. Miserably. It got so I hated walking into my office. It got so this memoir, this work that was supposed to help me write through my grief, was causing me even more misery. 'That's it!' I said finally. 'I'm done!' At least I *thought* I was." Mrs. Morice-Gilland stopped for a couple of seconds—and it seemed to me that she was doing it for dramatic effect, the way my dad used to when he'd read to me. That's when I realized she was *enjoying* this. That telling a story was the thing she loved most in the world.

"Then, one night, I couldn't sleep. . . . well, *most*

nights I couldn't sleep. I was always so aware of that empty space where Edward used to be that it would keep me up half the night. Anyway, I turned on the lamp, thought I'd read or knit, but instead I reached over to the bookcase and picked up a yellow legal pad and a pen. I don't know why I did, but I did. And I started drawing. Now, sketching had been quite an obsession of mine when I was young. I didn't just write my own stories, I illustrated them, too, but I hadn't drawn a thing since I was twelve or thirteen. But that night . . ." Her eyes just kind of lit up, and for a second, it was almost like it wasn't an old woman sitting across from me, but a little girl. "That night I didn't even think about it. My hand started moving, and the first thing that hit the page was this elephant-headed, fat-bellied, gentle-souled creature. Oh, I could see right away where the inspiration came from. He was part Ganesha and part Buddha. But something more. Something unique."

This was the part I really wanted to hear. Imagos, too, I guess, because he leaned way forward in his chair. I scooted closer to Mrs. M-G—but not *too* close. I couldn't tell what Gerald Epstein was thinking. He seemed kind of uncomfortable and kept moving around in his chair (maybe it was too small for him).

Mrs. Morice-Gilland went on with her story. "'Who

are you?' I asked . . . and the elephant started talking to me. I swear, I could hear his voice in my head, telling me all about himself, about Imaginalis. . . ." She looked over at the Prince again. "About you, Prince Imagos, and Rajah Merogji and Pralaya, and I wrote it all down. No, no, no—*Nossyss* wrote it! I was just taking dictation!"

"I don't think," the Prince said, "that Uncle had anything to do with it."

"With all respect, Your Highness," Mrs. Morice-Gilland said (she sure didn't talk to Imagos the way she talked to me or Mr. Epstein), "I beg to differ." She stopped and just stared at him again, then shook her head like she still couldn't believe what she was seeing. "The next night," she finally went on, "same thing. Only"—she pointed at Imagos—"I drew *you*. And next Pralaya emerged, in all his foul and wonderful glory. Then Prognostica, Yalee, Shokra, Wallawalla, your entire kingdom exploding in my mind." She looked out the window, but I had this feeling she was really looking all the way to Imaginalis. "It was extraordinary. I filled up pad after pad with notes. No, they weren't notes, they were *transmissions!* I'd be so exhausted after my scribbling that I'd sleep like a baby . . . and in the morning I'd look over what I'd written and it was almost as if I'd never seen it before."

She pushed herself up from the couch and started pacing again. "Every day I'd walk into my office, say good morning to you all, ask what you wanted to tell me about, and I'd listen. Not just listen. *See!* Movies playing in my mind. Your words, your actions, all laid out before me. Oh, I'd read about mystics and mediums who did automatic writing, and this was like that, I suppose. But better. So *much* better. All I had to do was take down what I saw, edit it, and I had the first book. Wrote it in three weeks. *Three weeks!*

"It was the same for the second and the third and the fourth. The series never did terribly well. Oh, well enough for them to publish the sequels, but we were always hanging on by a thread."

"I did my very best for you, Mikela," Epstein said— and he sounded really sorry.

The old woman stopped pacing, looked over at Epstein, and her expression was almost (I said almost) kind. "I know you did, Gerald. I know you did." She sighed, turned back to Prince Imagos. "Every time there was talk of a new contract, I held my breath, waiting for them to drop the ax. But in the end, *I* was the one who dropped it. Or maybe all of *you* were."

"Us?" the Prince asked—and he sounded confused by that. And maybe a little insulted, too.

"You," she said, nodding, that deep sadness back in her eyes. "I signed the contract for the fifth book, and . . ." It was pretty clear she didn't want to go on, but she knew she had to. "*Nothing*. No pictures. No words. I kept calling you all, begging you to talk to me . . . but you refused."

"Maybe," I piped in, "that was because they were all in Nolandia. Maybe their stories couldn't reach you from there."

She didn't snap at me or give me *that look*. Just nodded her head. "Or maybe my own writer's block is what sent them to Nolandia in the first place. We'll never really know, will we? Whatever the case," she went on, "my deadline came and went. I got an extension. That came and went. I told them I'd had a brilliant insight, a new theme, a host of new characters and needed a few more months to restructure the story. Then *that* deadline came and went." She stopped by the piano, poked at a few of the keys. "When the company told me that the sales were just too low and that they were canceling the series, I was actually relieved."

I couldn't help myself. "Why didn't you *fight* for it?" I said. "Why didn't you take it to another publisher? Why didn't you do *something*?"

Mrs. Morice-Gilland sat down in the window seat.

Closed her eyes. All of a sudden her voice sounded weak and tired. Like she was a thousand years old. "Why put myself through that agony? Whatever door had been opened in my mind . . . was closed tight. I couldn't write a word."

"But you're *the Dreamer*, you *created* Imaginalis. You should have been able—"

"I," Mrs. M-G snapped (but it felt kind of like she was snapping more at herself than me), "created *nothing*. I was just a radio dial, lucky enough to tune in to the right station." Her voice got softer. She looked out the window again. "There's the question, isn't it? Did *I* dream Imaginalis? Or did Imaginalis dream *me* dreaming *it*?"

"Or maybe," I said, excited, "each world dreamed the other!"

"Or," Prince Imagos said with the sweetest smile, "perhaps Something Bigger dreamed us *all* into being?"

"You mean the Silver Queen?" I asked.

"That's *one* name for her," Imagos said quietly. "One of many." He walked across the room, sat down at the window seat next to Mrs. Morice-Gilland. Took her hand. "Do you think," he asked, "you can help us? Join your belief to Mehera's, dream us an Unbelievable Bridge that won't carry us just across the worlds but into a reborn—a new and better—Imaginalis?"

"I'm afraid," Mrs. Morice-Gilland answered, "that my days of dreaming are over."

"I disagree, Mikela," Gerald Epstein said. His voice sounded different. I couldn't quite figure out how. It just sounded . . . *wrong*, somehow. Maybe he'd sounded that way all along, but I sure hadn't noticed it. Whatever it was, something in the way he was talking made my chest get all tight. "I think," Epstein went on, pushing up from his chair, "the two of you are more than capable of bringing Imaginalis back to life." I looked over at the Prince, and he had this look in his eyes, like he was suddenly figuring out something he should have already known. He jumped to his feet, just as—

The whole room was filled with this *horrendous* stink. Epstein started to shake, so hard I thought he was having a seizure or something. Then these bubbles started forming on his face and arms like he was kind of boiling from the inside out—and whole chunks of his skin started dripping and oozing onto the floor like candle wax. That was weird enough (and take my word for it, weird doesn't begin to cover it), but then his eyes . . . *his eyes came loose and slid down his face* and his entire body *exploded*—just like a volcano—and then . . .

It wasn't a body at all anymore. Not a human one,

anyway. It was this humongous ball of the most disgusting slime you could ever imagine, with *dozens* of crazy eyes just sort of rolling around in all that thick gunk. The whatever-it-was let out a howl that nearly blew out my eardrums, and then these snake-headed tentacle thingies busted through its chest (if it actually had a chest—I'm not sure it did), wriggling all over the place, their jaws snapping in every direction. I put my hand over my mouth. Between the stink of that thing and the look of it, it took all I had not to puke up every meal I'd eaten in twelve years.

We all knew who it was . . . *what* it was . . . but Mrs. Morice-Gilland was the first one to name it: *"Pralaya!"* the old woman cried.

The eyes in that pulsing mound of yuck swam around and around for a few seconds; then six or eight of them fixed themselves on Mrs. Morice-Gilland. "Yes," it said, in a voice that was even more sickening than that horrible stench. "Yes," it repeated.

CHAPTER TWENTY-TWO
Pralaya

"*Mehera, take cover!*" Imagos shouted. I stood there, so scared I couldn't move, wondering where, exactly, you hide from a monster in an old lady's living room, when the Prince reached for the quiver on his back and shot off three or four Eternity Arrows—so fast I could hardly even see them—straight at Pralaya.

A bunch of those tentacle thingies started wriggling around, forming some kind of weird symbol in the air that looked a little like the Egyptian hieroglyphs we learned about in history, only *made out of fire*. The Arrows smashed into the symbol, then exploded backward, slamming into the Prince. There was this incredibly loud, incredibly hot explosion. It felt like the temperature in the room went up about a thousand degrees—and for a second I couldn't see anything. But I could sure feel the blast—throwing me across the room.

I hit something. Hard.

When I could see again, I found myself on the floor, under the piano, flat on my back—and Prince Imagos was floating in the air above me, trapped in this shimmery cage that looked like it was made of the same fiery energy that the hieroglyph was. "Your Majesty," I asked, "are you all right?"

"Yes, Mehera," he said. But he didn't look all right. He looked like Pralaya's attack had really hurt him.

I looked over and saw that Mrs. M-G was on the floor, just a couple of feet away from me. She looked worse than the Prince. "Mrs. Morice-Gilland?"

The old woman nodded. She looked confused for a second—like she wasn't even sure where she was—but then she got *that look* in her eyes again, the same one she'd used on me and Mr. Epstein. "Is this how you greet your creator?" she asked Pralaya—and she didn't sound scared in the least. In fact, if she'd used that tone of voice on me, I would have been shaking in my Doc Martens.

That oozing ball of sewage kind of crawled over toward Mrs. Morice-Gilland. It laughed—the sound was exactly the way Mrs. M-G described it in *Flight from Forever*: like molten lava—and said, "A moment ago you told us . . . that you had nothing to do with the creation of Imaginalis. That the story came to you . . . flowed through you . . . and now you have the arrogance . . . to call yourself my creator?"

The old woman got slowly to her feet—and you could tell it wasn't easy for her. "Perhaps we'll never know how it really happened," she said. "But in some way, I *did* create you. You were born out of my grief and anger. A widow's bitterness and rage."

"Bitterness," that mountain of gunk said, and it seemed to enjoy saying the word. "Rage." It made this sickening gurgling sound, like a toilet getting ready to overflow. "Perhaps your darkness called to me . . . and mine to you. Perhaps your books came to be . . . because we're so much alike, you and I. We are . . . collaborators."

"Ridiculous," Prince Imagos said. "You're just one small part in a far greater story, Pralaya. What called to Mrs. Morice-Gilland, what inspired her tales, was the glory of Imaginalis."

A dozen eyes rolled around in that yuck. Some of them seemed to be laughing at the Prince (y'know, if an eye could laugh), some of them were angry. A few of them seemed like they just plain hated Imagos. "I don't recall . . . asking you to speak . . . Your Majesty."

"And I don't recall inviting you to accompany us to this world." The Prince grabbed the bars of his cage—there was this big fiery spark; for a second I could smell burning skin—and Imagos let go. "How did you do it, Pralaya?" he said. "How did you get here?"

Pralaya kind of just stood there—not that it had any legs—bubbling and oozing for a while. "*Mehera* brought me here," it finally said.

"Liar!" I shouted. Then all those awful eyes stared straight at me, and I was sorry I'd opened my Big Dumb Mouth.

"Oh, yes, Mehera," Pralaya answered, "I *am* a liar. An extraordinarily skilled one." It crept toward me, and that terrible stink got even worse. "But this time . . . I'm telling the truth. You carried me here . . . without realizing it. You couldn't help it. You see . . . I'm such a vital . . . such a necessary . . . part of the Imaginalis stories . . . that your belief in *me* . . . is as strong as your belief in *them*." The big ball of gunk shook all over, kind of like Jell-O, and those eyes started spinning around. It made me dizzy just to look at them. "One moment I was in Nolandia . . . that damnable lion watching my every move . . . and the next that belief grabbed hold of me. Carried me across the Unbelievable Bridge and into your world."

"That's not possible," I said, backing away.

"I'm afraid it is," Prince Imagos said.

I turned to the Prince. "I—I'm so sorry. I didn't mean to—"

Imagos smiled—and I could tell, right away, that he didn't blame me at all (which was incredibly nice, considering it was my fault he was sitting there, trapped in a cage). "It's all right, Mehera. My father used to tell me that some things are simply meant to be. And for reasons we don't understand yet, Pralaya is meant to be here." The Prince turned back to Pralaya. "And Yalee? Where is he?"

"Still back there, I assume," Pralaya replied. "The girl's belief clearly didn't extend to him." I knew he was probably right. Since Yalee's character showed up in the books only once in a while—and he wasn't exactly my favorite when he did—I never really *connected* with him the way I did with the others. In fact, I couldn't really understand why Yalee was even still around in Nolandia. Why he hadn't become a shadow like the other Imaginalians. I mean, Nossys and Prognostica and the Prince were only there because I so totally believed in them.

And hard as it was for me to admit it, I totally believed in Pralaya, too. I mean, he was in the books as much as Prince Imagos—and sometimes he was an even bigger part of the story. Even when he *wasn't* around, he was the character all the other characters would always plot against and talk about. How could I *not* believe in him?

All of a sudden, that blubbery mountain of sewer gunk started shaking—so hard I thought it was going to blow apart (and, believe me, I didn't want that yuck splattering all over me)—and then its tentacle thingies kind of whipped back into the center of the gunk, its eyes getting sucked down after them. It was like Pralaya was a big ball of clay and it was molding itself. *Reshaping* itself. That super-deluxe barf-bag stink began to fade away, and then the whole room started smelling like some kind of sickeningly sweet perfume that was just as bad (well, almost).

Then the monster was gone, and there was a woman standing there. Her hair was the same bright red as the *man* version of Pralaya that I'd met in Nolandia, but really long now, hanging down close to the floor. Her eyes were that same amazing blue, but they were wider now, ringed with blue eye shadow and black eyeliner. The woman's skin was white and perfect, and her lips were painted a shade of red that matched her hair *exactly*. She was wearing this dress that was kind of like an Indian sari—but not—and a silk shawl that was almost as blue as her eyes. The truth is, she was *absolutely beautiful*. "Forgive me," Pralaya—well, the woman who used to be Pralaya—said, in this really soft, sweet voice. "I sometimes forget that your human senses are unable to

Pralaya sighed. "I've been watching you all for some time: becoming a student at Mehera's school, a butterfly fluttering by the tree house, a cardinal alighting outside the kitchen window. So many forms." All of a sudden, I remembered that redheaded boy at Queenstown Family, and my whole stomach kind of turned over. "Watching and listening and learning. I thought your idea," she said, turning to look at me, "to find our dear Mr. Epstein was an excellent one. And so I made it my business to get to his office before you. I drained whatever information I needed from Gerald's bewildered little brain, assumed his shape, and then sent him off to a hotel. When he wakes up . . . and it may take a week . . . his head will be pounding, and he'll be sick to his stomach but otherwise unharmed."

"But what is it that you want?" Mrs. M-G asked.

"Ah, yes," Pralaya said, smiling. "You understand, don't you, Mikela? To be interesting, a character, especially a great villain like myself, must have an overriding desire, a *need* that must be fulfilled. And what I want," she went on, "is to stay right here."

"In my *house?*" Mrs. Morice-Gilland asked.

"In your *world*," Pralaya said.

"If you've been spying on us," Prince Imagos said, "then you know that's impossible. We weren't made for this world. It's . . . infecting us. If we don't return to

Imaginalis, we'll die here."

Pralaya looked up at the Prince with this really obnoxious expression on his face, kind of like he felt sorry for Imagos or thought he was some kind of idiot. "*You'll* die here, not me."

"What do you mean?" I asked.

"As you are well aware," Pralaya answered, "your Earth is a place of endless terrors. Your lives are fragile, your hearts full of fear. The very planet itself is struggling to survive all that humankind has done to it." She looked over at Imagos. "No, son of Merogji, you *don't* belong here. But this place"—she laughed, but there was nothing funny about it—"was *made* for me. Each day, each moment I stay here, I grow stronger. And in time—"

"In time?" Imagos asked.

"Oh," Pralaya said, yawning, reaching her arms over her head, "the possibilities are endless." She stood up, straightened her shawl. "All it will take is a little push here, some small encouragement there. A hurricane." And suddenly we weren't in that room anymore, we were *inside a storm*. We *were* the storm. And I could feel Pralaya's mind, all around us, controlling it. "A famine." Then we were in Africa somewhere, I think, and a little girl was really sick. Starving. And her hunger. *Her hunger was Pralaya.* "A tsunami." We were a wave, rising up, wiping out an entire island. "A war." Guns were going off all around us. Bombs were exploding. But the hate in the air, that was the worst of all. *And that was Pralaya, too.* "I'll simply speed things up a little, and this entire planet will collapse into chaos. Give me ten years . . . no, *five* . . . and I'll rule this planet without having to wage a single battle." Her eyes sparkled. "But first, of course, there's all of you to deal with."

The woman turned to Mrs. Morice-Gilland. "It's a wonderful story, don't you think? The dreaded Pralaya finally defeats Prince Imagos, utterly destroys Imaginalis, and finds a new world, a new *kingdom*, to rule. It could be the next . . . the *final* . . . chapter in your Imaginalis series."

"It would," Mrs. Morice-Gilland said, "make quite a book."

"What?" I yelped. "How can you say that? This isn't some story. It's really happening."

Before Mrs. Morice-Gilland could snap at me—and I was pretty sure that she was going to—Pralaya said, "What did Prognostica tell you, Mehera, when you had your little sleepover?" That's when I knew the annoying gnat that was buzzing around my room that night had been Pralaya. "'The whole universe is just a story.' For once the Nebulous Seer was right. Whether we're aware of it or not, all of us are characters in a cosmic tale. All of us have our roles to play."

"You make it sound like life's just some kind of game," I said.

"In a way it is," Pralaya answered.

"So in this story," I asked, "it's *your* role to—what? Hurt people? Make them suffer?"

For a second it looked like Pralaya was getting angry, but either I was wrong or she managed to control herself. "Someone has to. And that someone is me." She took two steps toward me, and I took two steps back. Way back. "I'm not evil, Mehera. I'm simply playing my part. Doing what's expected of me."

"What's expected of you?" Prince Imagos said. He was really angry. Angrier than I'd ever seen him. "Before you assassinated my father, before my mother died of a broken heart and our kingdom fell before your armies . . . *our lives were perfect.* We were living in a Golden Age."

Pralaya ignored the Prince and just kept looking at me. "*Were* they?" she asked. "Tell me, Mehera, what good is a Golden Age if you don't appreciate the gold?" The woman suddenly disappeared, so fast it scared me, and that stinking pile of slime was there again. "Snatch it away . . . break it apart, and then . . . when it's restored . . . it will finally be appreciated," Pralaya growled. "Or should

I say *if* it's restored . . . don't assume there'll be a happy ending this time."

"Oh," Prince Imagos said, "we'll have our happy ending, Pralaya. But we don't need a murdering liar like *you* to help us find it."

Pralaya laughed, really gently, and I realized that the woman form was back again. So fast I hadn't even noticed her change. "You'll never be rid of me," she said. "Down through the endless ages. Since the dawn of Imaginalis, I've risen again and again, haven't I? Smashed your towers, murdered your rajahs, burned your joy to the ground. Which means, of course, that you *need* me."

"I most certainly do not," Imagos said.

"Perhaps *you* don't—but *she* does," Pralaya said, pointing at me. "Our beloved audience."

"Me?" I said. "*I* don't need you."

"If you don't need me," Pralaya answered, "then why did you call me here, across the Bridge?"

I didn't have an answer for that one.

"You called me," the woman went on, "because I'm important. You called me because you know that day needs night. Light needs shadow. *And every story needs a villain.* Without me, the Imaginalis series would be the most exquisitely boring story ever told. But *with* me—" she said, turning toward the cage. "Look how exciting things are now! You're trapped here with the great and terrible Pralaya . . . your hero, Prince Imagos, locked in a cage and unable to help you. Will you escape? Or will I destroy you all? Be honest, Mehera. This is the way you want it."

The weird part was, she was right. I mean, most of the stories I've ever read have all played out that way: Stop the bad guy, end the war. And the fun was always in the fight. The big battle for control of Middle Earth. The good Narnians against the White Witch. Harry Potter facing Lord Voldemort, with the fate of the whole wizarding world in the balance. That's what made the stories so much *fun*. But I didn't . . . I couldn't . . . admit that to Pralaya. "That's—that's not true," I said. And I felt ashamed for lying. Even to Pralaya.

"You don't sound very sure of yourself."

"Well, I am," Prince Imagos shouted. I turned toward the cage just as he reached for his belt, and all of a sudden, he had a *sword* in his hand. It must have been four feet long, and it was glowing, really bright, with this bright green light. At first I couldn't figure it out. The sword hadn't been there the second before. But then I remembered that in *Escape to Nolandia*, the Prince had been given a sword. It was called the Blade of Need. And it was a sword that could be used only once, just once in Imagos's entire life, when the need was greatest. It would hang on his belt, invisible, till he was ready to use it.

And I guess he was ready.

I jumped up and down and cheered when Imagos used the sword to slice the bars of the cage totally apart. Cheered even louder when he jumped down to the floor and raced toward the woman. Pralaya threw up a few more of those fiery hieroglyphs, but Imagos just swatted at them with the sword and they blew apart, throwing the woman back against the wall. Only she wasn't a woman anymore, she was that stinky, blobby monster, its tentacle thingies thrashing around, trying to get at Imagos. But the Blade of Need couldn't be stopped. As quick as those tentacles shot out, Imagos cut them away. It took maybe ten seconds before he had the monster trapped there, the sword pressed against it. "I have waited all my life for this moment," the Prince said. He raised up the sword, and I knew, I just knew, that with one stroke Pralaya would be finished forever. But the Prince had this *really weird* look in his eyes, and it kind of scared me. It was almost like he wasn't Imagos at all anymore. Or maybe he was an Imagos I never, ever wanted to see.

Something about that look made me remember something. Something really important. "Your Highness," I shouted. "*Don't!*"

The Prince whirled. "Mehera, what—?" was all he could say.

"Don't you remember what your father said, in *Flight from Forever*?"

The Prince just looked at me like I was crazy. Then I realized that *he'd* never read the book; he'd *lived* it. "In—in the Forever Forest, I mean. When Rajah Merogji came to you. 'Compassion, not brutality,' your father said. 'That's the Imaginalian way.' He doesn't want you to defeat Pralaya this way. He wants you to aim for the impossible, and—"

A tentacle thingy wrapped around Imagos's throat, lifted him up. Another fiery symbol appeared in the air, and then there was an terrible explosion of heat and light and a sound so loud I shrieked and—

Prince Imagos flew back, smashing into the wall.

Pralaya—she was a woman again—stood there smiling, energy just kind of dancing across the palms of her hands.

"What did you do?" I screamed, rushing to Imagos's side. He was just staring up at the ceiling, but I had the feeling he was looking someplace else. Someplace way beyond that room. His chest was burned . . . it was actually smoking . . . in the place where Pralaya's spell had hit him.

"I'm sorry, I'm sorry, I'm so sorry," I said. "I was trying

to help. I only wanted you to do what your father—" I started crying. "Oh, God, this is all my fault. I brought Pralaya here and now I've—"

Prince Imagos shook his head. "No, Mehera." He tried to say something else, then coughed—I could see how much pain he was in—and started again. "There is . . . a *reason* for this. A reason—" He raised his hand— it was shaking *really* bad—and touched my face, pulling me closer. Then he whispered two words to me—I wasn't sure, but they sounded like "*Don't believe. . . .*" And then his hand kind of went limp and fell. He made this horrible rattling sound in his throat, I'll never forget it as long as I live, and then he stopped moving. Stopped breathing. Stopped everything. For a second his body got kind of wavery, kind of like those heat trails you see on the highway in the summer, and then he was just . . . gone.

I jumped up and ran straight at Pralaya. "What did you *do?*" I screamed again. Pralaya hit me . . . she hit me, *hard*, right across my face. No one had ever hit me before in my entire life. It was horrible. I fell back and down, sliding across the floor.

"What did I do?" Pralaya smiled. "What's *expected* of me."

CHAPTER TWENTY-THREE
Breaking

The next thing I remember, Mrs. Morice-Gilland was down on the floor next to me, putting her arms around me. I was confused and I couldn't think straight and my whole body felt so cold I was shaking. "Mehera?" Mrs. M-G said quietly.

I leaned my head against her shoulder. "I don't understand," I said. "Has he gone back across the Bridge? To Nolandia?"

"No," Mrs. Morice-Gilland whispered. "Someplace far beyond Nolandia, I think. And I'm afraid he's never coming back. I'm sorry, Mehera."

"As am I," Pralaya said, walking over to us. "Not that you'd ever believe me. I admired that boy. One day he might have been even greater than his father."

"Then why," I asked her, "did you kill him?"

"Because," she answered, sitting on the floor next to us, tucking her legs up underneath her, "the Prince was the only one left with power to oppose me."

"Lord Nossyss will stop you," Mrs. Morice-Gilland said. She sounded like she was trying to convince herself as much as Pralaya.

"Lord Nossyss," Pralaya answered, "can do nothing. And very soon he will *be* nothing. The old elephant will fade as surely as the Prince did. And soon after that, Prognostica will follow. There will be no one left to save the Imaginalians. The entire kingdom will be engulfed in the darkness of Nolandia. Erased. *Forgotten.*"

"No!" I shouted. "I'll never forget! *Never!*"

"That *is* a problem, Mehera," Pralaya answered. "My biggest problem. You just *might* still remember. Your connection to Imaginalis is so strong that somewhere, deep in your mind, just the hint of knowledge, the whisper of memory, may survive. But even one small whisper is far too dangerous."

I looked over at Mrs. Morice-Gilland. "We'll *both* remember," I said. "I know we will."

"*Her?*" Pralaya said, looking at Mrs. M-G like she actually felt sorry for her. "Soon, I'm afraid, she won't remember anything." Mrs. Morice-Gilland got this horrible look on her face, like she was more afraid than she'd ever been in her life. Then she closed her eyes and turned away from us.

"What are you talking about?" I asked.

"She's *old*, Mehera," Pralaya said. "Oh, not old for my world. But for yours? Ancient beyond imagining. And she's sick. Riddled with disease. Another few months—two, three at best—and she'll be as much a faded memory as the others. No threat to me at all."

"Is—is that true, Mrs. Morice-Gilland?" I asked. "Are you . . . ?"

Mrs. Morice-Gilland turned to back to me, and she looked sadder than I'd ever seen her. No, it wasn't that she was sad; it was more like she'd just given up. "Yes, Mehera, it's true."

"But can't you . . . ?"

"I've had all the treatments I can bear. They're worse than the disease." She tried to smile, but she couldn't quite get it to work. "It's my time," she said.

For the second time that day, I felt something way deep inside of me . . . something old and dark and scary. It kept pushing at me and pushing at me—but I wouldn't let it out. I *couldn't* let it out.

"So you see, Mehera," Pralaya went on, "*you* are my sole concern. A human with the spark of the Silver Queen, with the capacity to dream, the ability to bridge the worlds. Given time, you might actually find a way to pull them out of Nolandia."

"I will," I said. "I'll never stop trying."

Pralaya stood up, arched her back, and stretched out her arms. "I could," she said, "weave a spell, burying Imaginalis inside you, beneath layers of thought, oceans of memory. But I could never bury it completely. And I'm prevented from simply taking it; your personal magic is too great. The Silver Queen's spark is too bright." She stopped for a few seconds, like she was enjoying dragging this out, and then said, "But there *is* another way."

"What way?" Mrs. Morice-Gilland asked.

Pralaya ignored the old woman and just kept looking right at me. "You're going to *give* your memories of Imaginalis to me, Mehera. Willingly. As a gift."

"Yeah, right," I said, "like that's ever gonna happen."

"Oh, it is," Pralaya said. With her index finger, she outlined a circle on her forehead, then tapped it three times. A mindfire, a small black bubble of thought, pushed through and popped out into the air. But this wasn't like any of the mindfires I'd seen before. I watched it get bigger until it was the size of a beach ball. And there was something inside it . . . an *image*, slowly coming into focus, like one of those old television sets that take forever to turn on. "It is," Pralaya said again, as the image got clearer—and then I saw my father, right there inside the mindfire. Well, he wasn't really in there, he was in A Thousand Voices, sitting behind the counter, reading a book.

"Papa?" I said. My voice was shaking.

"Papa," Pralaya repeated.

"Is this," Mrs. Morice-Gilland asked, "happening *now*, or—?"

"An excellent question from the insightful author," Pralaya answered. "No," she went on, "this isn't now. But it's soon, Mehera. Very soon." In the mindfire, my father made this face, like he was in pain all of a sudden. His shoulders hunched forward. His hand went to his chest. He kind of staggered off the stool, leaning on a book display. It fell over—and then so did he. He was flat on the floor.

And he wasn't moving.

My mind felt like *it* was on fire. And my heart, too. It was horrible enough watching Prince Imagos die, learning that Mrs. Morice-Gilland would going to die soon, too—but *this*? My *father*? "Papa!" I screamed—at least I tried to. It came out like a whisper.

"Such fragile creatures, you humans," Pralaya said. "So many ways to die. Something goes wrong in the brain." She snapped her fingers. "Gone. A problem in the heart." Snapped again. "Gone. A slip in the shower, a car accident, an undiagnosed illness." Pralaya moved the mindfire gently from palm to palm. "An undiagnosed illness," she said again. "Isn't that what happened with your mother, Mehera? She waited too long to get the tests." Inside the mindfire, the image changed. Papa was gone, and now there was an ugly little hospital room. And there was a woman there, in the bed. She was so skinny, she almost looked like a skeleton, and she was hooked up to all kinds of tubes and wires and machines.

"Stop," I tried to say—and this time the word wouldn't come out at all.

"She didn't feel quite right, but she kept putting it off and putting it off until . . ." Pralaya flicked the mindfire into the air and snapped her fingers again. "Gone."

"*Stop!*" I shrieked. I jumped up, ran after the mindfire. I wanted to destroy it, pop it like a balloon, make it—and that horrible, horrible picture *inside* it—go away forever. But something stopped me. I just stood there, not moving, a couple of inches away from it. Staring at my mother, at what the cancer had *left* of my mother. And then I reached out my hands. The mindfire drifted down, like it knew what I wanted, and I held it against my chest. Dropped to my knees. And cried and cried and cried. "Mama," I said through my tears. "Mama."

It's not like I hadn't cried about my mother before. I did when I was little, I cried a lot. And it's not like I didn't ever miss her. I did sometimes. I missed her a lot. But it wasn't until right then that I realized all the tears I hadn't *let* myself cry, all the missing I hadn't let myself *feel*. I'd been pretending for so long that I was okay, that it was no big deal that my mother had died, that it was so long ago it didn't matter. But it *did* matter. It mattered more than anything on any world in any universe.

"Mama," I sobbed, over and over and over again. "*Mama, Mama, Mama, Mama.*"

"Stop it!" Mrs. Morice-Gilland shouted. "Leave her *alone*, you soulless, evil—"

Pralaya looked over at the old woman. "You can't lay this at *my* feet," she said softly. "I didn't create *this* pain. Blame whoever dreamed your Earth into being. Whoever wrote the pathetic story of your lives."

Mrs. Morice-Gilland didn't say anything. She just got up and shuffled to the window. It seemed like it took her forever. She stood there for a while, then bowed her head, kind of like she was praying. I didn't know what she was doing over there, and I really didn't care. The only thing that mattered to me was that mindfire. I wanted to hold on to it, hold on to *her*, for as long as I could. "*Mama . . .*"

Pralaya walked across the floor and looked down at me. "I can't change what happened to your mother, Mehera," she said quietly. "That magic is too great for me, too great for anyone. But I *can* protect your father. You won't lose him the way you lost her." She leaned over, wiped the tears from my cheeks with the blue shawl. "Just give me the memories I want, and he'll be with you for years and years to come. I promise you. I give you my sacred word." Pralaya tapped the mindfire gently. It slipped out of my hands and rose up, up, up and through the ceiling. And just like that it . . . *she* . . . was gone.

I sat there for the longest time. I cried until I didn't have any tears left, then I cried some more. "Okay," I finally said, looking up at Pralaya. "I'll give them to you."

I looked across the room at Mrs. Morice-Gilland, but she was still standing there with her head bowed and eyes closed. Her lips were moving, but there wasn't any sound.

Pralaya reached out and wrapped her hands around my head. "Thank you, Mehera," she said.

And that's when the winged lion broke through the door.

CHAPTER TWENTY-FOUR
The Beginning of the End

"How?" Pralaya howled, staring at the lion with a look of total amazement, and total panic, on her face.

Mrs. Morice-Gilland whirled around. "I called him," she said. "With *all my heart*, I called him." She turned to the lion with the man's face and smiled. "And I believed that you would come. Oh, how I *believed* it."

Yalee looked over at Mrs. M-G and bowed low. "That belief is what kept me from vanishing into the deeps of Nolandia," he said. "That belief carried me across the Bridge. That belief," he went on, turning back to the red-haired woman, "writes an end to Pralaya's story."

Yalee leaped across the room.

At first, I really wasn't sure what was happening: I thought the lion showing up was another of Pralaya's tricks. But then Yalee smashed into Pralaya, knocked her to the ground, and brought one of his gigantor paws down across her face. When I saw the blood, when I heard Pralaya scream and curse, I knew that this really *was* the winged lion and that he really *had* made his way across the worlds from Nolandia. Maybe I hadn't believed enough in Yalee—but Mrs. Morice-Gilland had enough belief for both of us.

"You," Yalee said, pinning Pralaya to the floor, "are finished. And this time, there will be no escape. This time"—his mouth opened up so wide, he could have swallowed half the room—"you will *stay* dead."

I knew I was safe now: Pralaya couldn't hurt me. So why did the sight of that blood and the sound of that awful screaming make me feel so sick and sad? Why did I want to run across the room and beg the lion to stop?

There was another hot blast, another loud boom, and Yalee was thrown back, skidding across the floor, his claws gashing the wood. Pralaya jumped to her feet, except there wasn't a "her" there. She . . . he . . . was a man now, the same Pralaya I'd first met in Nolandia. "We're not in Imaginalis anymore," he said, bolts of fiery sorcery exploding from his palms, hitting Yalee hard. There were wounds on the lion's side. One of his wings was all black. "The sorrow and suffering in this world feed me, make me stronger in a way you could never comprehend."

There was another blast, and Yalee roared in pain..

Pralaya raised his arms and blasted the lion again. At least he tried to. But Yalee was ahead of him this time, leaping across the room to me. "On my back, child," Yalee said. "We cannot stay here." Something bright and hot shot right past me—it probably would have hit me if the lion hadn't pushed me out of the way. "On my back," Yalee said again. He wasn't asking, he was telling.

I climbed on. "But what about Mrs. Morice-Gilland?"

"Don't worry about me," the old woman said. "Just go!"

"*No!*" I cried.

"Go!"

We flew—out the door and into the sky, with bursts of sorcery exploding all around us.

I looked down and saw Pralaya outside the house. He wasn't a man *or* a woman now, he was just a . . . thing, melting and oozing, dragging itself across the grass, leaving a trail of steaming slime gunk behind it. I saw another fiery hieroglyph form in the air, and then it changed, turning into some kind of circular platform that the Pralaya thing crawled onto.

The platform shot straight up into the sky.

He was right behind us.

And now you know how I ended up, scared half to death (but thrilled, too—in a stomach-turning kind of way), sailing over the North Carolina woods, riding a winged lion across the sky. Chased by a living nightmare that wanted to destroy me.

"Always follow your dreams," my mother used to tell me. "They may not lead you where you expect to go, but they'll always lead you someplace wonderful." Well, I'd followed my dreams, and they'd led me someplace that didn't feel wonderful at all.

I turned to see if the nightmare was still behind us, and something hit me like a flamethrower in the face. The pain was terrible. It burned my skin, it burned my mind. I think it might have burned my soul.

The mane slipped from my hands.

The lion roared.

I was falling.

Something warm and wet wrapped itself around me. At first I panicked, tried to fight it off, sure it was Pralaya—but then I realized that it was Yalee, and that he was holding me *in his mouth*. I should have been terrified—well, okay, I *was*; one slip of those teeth and I would have been Mehera Beatrice Shishkabob—but when I looked in Yalee's eyes, saw the way he looked at me, I knew then that he'd take care of me, do everything in his power to keep me safe.

The lion spread his wings wide and glided down, landing in a clearing in the middle of some woods. I didn't know if we were five miles from Mrs. Morice-Gilland's house or five hundred. Yalee leaned forward, sort of rolling me down onto the ground. "I'm sorry, Mehera," he said. "But given the speed with which you were falling, I didn't think I could manage to get you onto my back. Catching you in my mouth seemed to be the best choice."

I got to my feet. "Yeah, well," I said. It wasn't much of an answer, but it was all I could come up with. I was tired, I was hungry, I was confused, I was scared. And my right cheek was burning. I touched it but pulled my hand away fast. The wound was raw. The tiniest bit of pressure from my fingers hurt so bad I almost screamed.

Yalee padded over to me. "Let me look at that," he said, those man eyes underneath the lion's mane looking me over like he was a doctor giving me a physical. "You're lucky," he said.

"Lucky?" I said, wincing. The pain was getting worse

now. My cheek was throbbing.

"Pralaya's spell only grazed you," Yalee answered. He nuzzled his face in close; his breath smelled awful. "Hold still," he whispered.

"What are you do—" I started to say, but, before I could finish, the lion's tongue was sliding across my cheek, thick gobs of saliva running down my face. For a moment, there was an awful stinging—and then this funny tingling. I could feel, *actually feel*, my skin healing. No, it wasn't just healing. It was like the burn had never even happened. I suddenly remembered that, in the Imaginalis books, Yalee's Kiss—that's what Mrs. Morice-Gilland called it—had healing powers. What he'd given me wasn't exactly a kiss, but I guess Yalee's Slobber probably wouldn't have sounded as good.

I touched my face—there was no pain at all—and smiled. "Thank you, Yalee," I said. Okay, so the lion still kind of made me nervous (well, he pretty much terrified me), but he'd just saved my life. The least I could do was be polite. "What do we do now?" I asked him.

Yalee circled me. "First order of business," he said, checking the woods, on the lookout for any danger, "is to get you someplace safe, where Pralaya can't find you."

"But what about Mrs. Morice-Gilland? We can't just *leave* her back there."

The lion turned around and pushed his face close to me. This time his breath was so disgusting I almost gagged. "We'll see to Mrs. Morice-Gilland later," he said. "I promise. Now climb onto my back. Time is short, and we must get you to safety."

"But *Pralaya*," I said. "He's the greatest dark magician in Imaginalis. He can find us *anywhere*."

"True, true," the lion answered, like he'd never even thought of that. Then Yalee's eyes lit up. "I have an idea," he went on. "It's dangerous—more to *me* than you, but—"

"What do you mean?" I asked.

"Pralaya wants your memories of Imaginalis, correct?"

"Yes."

"But if you *didn't have* those memories," the lion went on, walking back and forth across the clearing, "he wouldn't even *bother* with you, would he? You wouldn't be a threat to him at all."

"I don't understand."

He turned to face me. "Give *me* the memories, Mehera. Keep them safe *in my mind*."

"What? Can you do that?"

"Yes. Only for a short time—when it comes to magic, my skills are woefully limited—but I'm hoping it will be long enough for me to *destroy* that filthy usurper once and for all."

"But," I said, "he's so much *stronger* here than he was in Imaginalis. You saw what happened back at the house. He'll kill you, Yalee."

The lion shook out his mane and roared. Really loud. "I have killed *him*, twice before," he said. "No one in all of Imaginalis can make that claim. I've killed him before, and I will do it again. And this time there will be no miraculous resurrection."

Suddenly I wasn't afraid of him anymore. All I knew was that I didn't want him . . . I didn't want anyone else . . . to die trying to protect me. I ran my hand through Yalee's mane and across his back. "I can't let you do it," I said.

"You must," the lion said. "Now climb onto my back, Mehera Crosby. There is no time to waste."

I was just about to climb up when something stopped me. Cold.

"What's wrong?" the lion asked.

"You were hurt," I said.

"What?"

"When Pralaya attacked you, in Mrs. Morice-Gilland's house. Your wing was burned. You had this big wound on your side."

"I healed myself," the lion answered quickly (a little too quickly, if you ask me). "Just as I healed *you*."

"But," I said, "in the books . . . in the books it says

that you *can't* heal yourself. That Yalee's Kiss can only help others, never—"

"The books," Yalee answered, "aren't always accurate, Mehera. Morice-Gilland can't get every detail right. Now come on," he said, and he sounded worried, "climb on my back before—"

I stepped back, suddenly remembering something else. "In Nolandia," I said quietly, "when we met . . ."

Yalee tilted his head. "What about it?"

"Your breath."

"My *breath*?" the lion growled.

"It smelled sweet. It smelled *wonderful*." I took three more steps back. "But now . . ."

He tapped a paw in the dirt like he was all nervous. "Mehera, this is *absurd*. We haven't the time for—"

"You're not Yalee," I said.

"You're still in shock, Mehera," the lion answered. "You're not making sense. Think, child. I *healed* you, didn't I? With my kiss? Only Yalee could do that."

I was scared—so scared I just wanted to run into the woods and keep going till I was thirty—but I wasn't going to let him stand there and lie to me like that. "*Sorcery* could do it, too."

Yalee didn't say anything. He just stared at me for a few seconds that felt more like a few million years.

"Why," he finally asked, raising himself up on his back legs, his body churning and bubbling, "do you have to make things so *difficult*?" Pralaya stood there now, its big fat lips sneering, every one of its eyes focused on me. "I wanted to make this *easy* for you."

That horrible smell came at me again, and this time I really did puke. "Where's Yalee?" I asked when I was done. "The *real* Yalee."

Three of those tentacle thingies pointed across the clearing, where Pralaya's platform suddenly appeared. The winged lion was flat on his back, his burned wings twitching, his eyes just staring up at . . . nothing. "Is he—?"

"No," Pralaya answered. "I saw no need . . . to kill him. As you said yourself . . . in *this* world . . . he's no threat to me. And soon enough . . . he'll be joining his friends . . . in Nolandia."

"And Mrs. Morice-Gilland?"

"Back at the cottage. The old fool . . . is no threat to me. Now come," the monster went on, slithering closer to me, "let's get this . . . over with."

"And," I asked, "if I don't give you my memories?"

Two dozen eyes closed, then opened again. Ten snakes wriggled and hissed. "Then," Pralaya said, "I suppose I'll have no choice but to *kill your father*."

CHAPTER TWENTY-FIVE
The Spark

"No!" I shouted. "Please!"

"Don't think . . . I *want* to do this," Pralaya said. "I only resort to murder . . . when absolutely necessary." The monster's form kind of bubbled and boiled, then changed again, turning back into the red-haired woman. But that didn't make me any less terrified. "But it's not going to come to that, Mehera," Pralaya said, "because I know you won't make me do it. I know you love your father too much to allow it."

And she was right. I would've given Pralaya everything I remembered, everything I knew, everything I *was*, if it meant Papa could live. But my father's life wasn't the only one on the line. "What about the Imaginalians?" I asked.

"Their time has passed," Pralaya said. "Let them go, let them fade." She had this smirk on her face, like she thought she was smarter, better, than me. Than everyone. "Really, what choice do you have?"

Truth was, I had no choice at all—unless one of the Imaginalians could help me. "Yalee!" I cried, rushing over to the platform, dropping down next to the lion, shaking him. In the books, he always showed up when the Imaginalians really, really needed him. It had always seemed a little fake to me, a little too easy—but, fake or not, I needed him now. Needed him more than I'd needed anyone ever before. "Yalee, get up—*please!*" The sun was setting now—it felt like it was setting on the whole world, forever—and the lion looked up at me, but I could tell he wasn't really seeing me. The poor thing tried, really hard, to lift his head, then slumped back.

I saw Pralaya coming for me and ran, fast as I could, across the clearing, looking up, past the tops of the trees. "Prognostica!" I screamed. "Uncle Nossyss! *Please!*"

"The old elephant," Pralaya said, "isn't going to descend from the heavens, amulet whirling, hands blazing with magic, to vanquish me."

"*He will!*"

Pralaya shook her head. "He's back in that tree house, slowly fading into oblivion. Don't you see, Mehera," she went on, "this isn't his world, and it isn't his story. It's *yours*. The very sad tale of Mehera Crosby, twelve years old, alone against a force she can never defeat."

"No," I said, refusing to believe it. "I know how these stories always turn out. Yalee *will* wake up. Or Uncle Nossyss. He'll find some cure for the Nolandia sickness and he'll stop you. Or Prince Imagos. I'll bet you just made us think he's dead, but he's not really, and he's gonna come charging in at the last minute and rescue me. I know he'll do it, because he's the hero. He's the *hero* and he's *got to*." But as soon as I said it, I knew it wasn't true.

"I know it hurts," the woman said, and she sounded like she really cared (not that I believed her for a second). "But once I take your memories of Imaginalis, you won't feel any pain."

For a second that idea—not feeling pain—sounded wonderful to me. That day, well, it was like I'd felt a whole *lifetime* of pain. Maybe if I asked, Pralaya would take it *all* away.

I think she could sense I was weakening. Pralaya nodded at me, her fingers wriggling like she couldn't wait to get her hands on me and suck out every last bit of Imaginalis. It would have been easy just to give up and surrender to her. It was like I'd been hanging off a cliff for hours and hours, hanging on to one tiny branch. I mean, wouldn't you, wouldn't anyone, just give up and fall?

Pralaya laughed. She sat down on the edge of the plat-form. Stretched out her legs. "You're getting older now," she said. "The time for fairy tales is long past. You're becoming a young woman—and young women don't read children's books. They don't believe in magic. They accept the world as it is. *They grow up.*" Those words, "grow up," had never sounded so mean. So ugly. "Maybe," Pralaya went on, "*that's* why you carried me over the Bridge, Mehera. Maybe that's why you brought me here. Because you knew it was time to let go of childish things. And you knew I was the one who could help you do it."

"No," I said, trying to sound sure of myself—but a part of me, a pretty big part, wondered if it was true.

"Yes," Pralaya answered. "Even your beloved Prince Imagos realized that as he died. 'Don't believe.' Those were his last words. The young fool saw the truth in the end. He saw things as they are, not as he wanted them to be. He gave up on his dreams of a Golden Age. A hopeful world. A *child's* world. You should, too." She ran her fin-gers through the lion's mane. "Don't believe, Mehera."

I wondered if that really was what Prince Imagos meant. Did he want me to give up, grow up, become one of those people who see rottenness and misery every-where they go? Who, probably because they lost their *own* dreams somewhere along the line, spend all their time ruining everyone else's? Hey, I may be twelve years old, but I'm not stupid. I know the world's not perfect, that it can hurt sometimes, hurt really bad. I learned that when I was seven, when Mama left me. But Mama left me something else, too: She showed me that life was good, that people were kind and decent and caring. She left a love in me that was even deeper than the Silver Queen's spark.

And Papa? He gave me love every morning for breakfast, every afternoon for lunch, every night for dinner, and then brought me more love for a bedtime snack.

But all of a sudden I realized that I couldn't just take that love for granted. I couldn't just think it was always going to be there. Because the CNN Reality, it's so big, so loud, so angry and ugly, that people—and monsters like Pralaya—think that's all there is. They can't see what's underneath, they can't see the hope and the magic and the love that's ten times, a gajillion times, bigger and more powerful than the CNN Reality will ever be.

But I couldn't blame anyone for not knowing that. Sometimes it was pretty hard to see. And I knew then, in a way I'd never known anything before, that the only way to *really* see it was to *choose it. Choose it every day.* Isn't that what Prognostica told me that night during our sleepover? That choosing was the most magnificent magic of all? And isn't that what Prince Imagos's last words really meant?

"Okay, Pralaya," I finally said. "You win. I won't believe."

Pralaya came toward me. "Good," she said. She tried to hide how excited she was, how hungry, but she couldn't. "You've made the right decision."

"And the *first* thing I won't believe in," I said, "*is you.*"

"What?"

"I won't believe . . . I *don't* believe . . . in you."

"Nonsense," Pralaya said, her hands reaching for me, her fingers twitching. "You have no power over me."

But just when Pralaya said that, I suddenly felt so *much* power that it nearly knocked me flat on my butt. It was like this tiny spark, way deep inside me, *the Silver Queen's spark*, had suddenly become a humongous fire. I swore I could actually feel her, feel the Silver Queen inside that fire, filling me up with her power. Guiding me—not with words, but with something else. Something deeper. And really wonderful.

I took a few steps forward, looked Pralaya right in the eyes, and shot her the most withering squint, the most devastating glare, I'd ever tried in my entire life.

And it worked.

Pralaya froze in her tracks.

"This is *my* world," I said, "*my* dream, my *story*—"

Pralaya rushed toward me, but the squint-glare—it was like some kind of invisible force field or something—held her back.

"And I choose not to have you in it!"

Pralaya just roared at me, but I wasn't afraid anymore.

"I don't believe in you," I said again. "Not in you! Not in anybody who wants to make life into something stupid and ugly and sad." My hand moved up to my head . . . but, in a weird way, it almost felt like it wasn't my hand at all. Like maybe it was the Silver Queen's hand inside mine. I (we?) drew a circle with my finger. Tapped three times. "But I *do* believe," I went on, and now even my voice sounded different, like I was Mehera and *not* Mehera at the same time, Imaginalian Queen and Queenstown Girl, speaking out of the same mouth, "in a new kind of story. A *better* story. For Earth . . . and for Imaginalis."

A man's head . . . his eyes were bugging out and he looked scared half to death . . . oozed up out of Pralaya's shoulder. "Mehera," he shrieked, "you called me here!" The woman's legs melted into a pile of waxy ooze, dozens of those creepy eyes swimming around in the muck. "Why would you do that if you didn't need me? If you didn't want me in your story?"

A mindfire—it looked kind of like a little moon—popped out of my forehead and sailed right at Pralaya, getting bigger and bigger as it went, becoming so ginormous that it totally surrounded him (or her, or it). That mindfire felt like it was filled with every kind thought I'd ever had. Every good thing I'd ever done. Every person I'd ever loved or cared about. Mama and Papa were in there. And so were Mrs. Young, Lasarina Webster, and Alana Sloane; Mia Clements, Aria Een, and Andrew Suarez. All the people from Queenstown Family. Every kid from school. (Even Laura Washington and Sheryl Bernstein. That sure surprised me. It was like I could suddenly see all the good in them, in a way I never could before.) And Celeste! I suddenly missed her so much, and I knew, just knew, that she really was, she'd always been, my very best friend in any world. "Maybe," I said, "there *was* another reason I called you over the Unbelievable Bridge—but I don't think I brought you here so you could help *me* change." All that love was inside the mindfire, getting brighter and brighter, washing over Pralaya, going down deep, into a heart that monster didn't even know it had. "I think it was so *I* could help *you*."

The mindfire's light got so bright that it hurt—and, for just a second (or maybe two), I swore I could see a woman—with sparkling wings, a diamond crown, and gorgeous shimmering skin—floating right there in the middle of the light. She put her fingers to her lips and blew me a kiss. And then the only thing I could *see* was light.

I looked away. I thought maybe my eyeballs would burn out if I didn't. And when I looked back, a few seconds later, the light was gone. And so was Pralaya. The only thing left was the mindfire. It was really small now, no bigger than a marble, a glowing, glittery ball that flew across the clearing and landed in the palm of my hand. I looked into the sparkling center of that ball, and I could *just* about make out a tiny form in there, flitting around like a firefly.

The little creature inside the mindfire made a sound, kind of like a wind chime, and I could feel it thanking me. "You're welcome, Pralaya," I said—and I knew then that it *was* Pralaya, a *new* Pralaya, a better one—and tucked the little mindfire into my vest pocket.

I heard a soft growl from across the clearing. The platform was gone. Yalee was lying there in the grass, groaning. He got up really slow. I could tell that it hurt.

"What happened?" he asked, limping over to me.

"I think the story's almost over," I said.

Almost—but not quite.

CHAPTER TWENTY-SIX
Word Magic

A few minutes later we were back at the cottage, and Mrs. Morice-Gilland was sitting on her couch, holding the tiny mindfire in her hands. "Do you realize what you've done, Mehera?" she asked me.

So much for being a hero. Now she was going to tell me how I'd totally screwed everything up. "No, ma'am," I said.

"Do you remember what Rajah Merogji told Prince Imagos, at the end of *Flight from Forever*? That he had to defeat Pralaya, but do it without violence? Without vengeance?"

"Of *course* I remember," I said. "That's what I was telling Imagos, just before he—"

"Don't interrupt," Mrs. Morice-Gilland snapped.

"Sorry." Having a life-or-death battle with Pralaya

was hard, but talking to this old lady was *really* dangerous.

"By transforming Pralaya," Mrs. M-G went on, "you
did *precisely* what the Rajah of the Swan instructed.
Brought down the enemy with compassion, not brutality. I had no idea how that could happen. . . . I was
terrified that I'd written myself into a corner . . . but
you . . ." She shook her head like she just couldn't believe
it. "You did it."

"I didn't do anything," I said. "It was the Silver
Queen."

"Did it even occur to you," Mrs. Morice-Gilland said,
"that what you *thought* was the Silver Queen was just the
deeper, the better, the truer part of *yourself*? That your
unconscious mind just manufactured the image of the
Silver Queen as a way to do something that is the very
essence of Imaginalis?" I had no clue what she was talking
about. "You pushed past your limits, Mehera. You aimed
for the impossible and hit the target, dead center."

"Are you saying," the lion growled (and he didn't
sound happy), "that our Silver Queen isn't real? That the
tales about her are lies?"

"Not at all," Mrs. Morice-Gilland answered. "I'm just
saying that the line between Silver Queens and little
girls, between gods and men, between who we *think*

we are and who we *really* are, is thinner than we can imagine."

The lion must have liked that answer, because he didn't growl again. "I still don't get it," I said.

"Let's just say that you helped create a new kind of story today. And Prince Imagos would have been proud."

We all got really quiet then, thinking about the Prince. I just couldn't believe he was really gone. "There must be some way," I said, "that we can bring him back."

"I'm afraid," Mrs. Morice-Gilland said, "that things don't work that way. On Earth or in Imaginalis."

And then I had the greatest idea in the History of Ideas. "I think they can," I said. "I think *you* can."

Mrs. Morice-Gilland looked at me like I was crazy. And maybe I was. But I'd finally figured out that there's good crazy and bad crazy—and this was definitely the good kind. "What are you talking about?" she asked. "What is it you think I can do?"

I looked over at the lion, then back at Mrs. Morice-Gilland. "Write Prince Imagos back to life," I said.

"*Write him back to life?*" Mrs. Morice-Gilland yelped. "Have you lost what little mind you have?"

I was so excited I could hardly stand still. "Don't you see?" I said. "You're his only hope. It was your imagination that created Prince Imagos. Who's to say you can't do it again?"

"Impossible," Mrs. M-G said. "I can't write him back to life. I—I can't write *anything*."

"You *have* to," I whined.

From the look on the old woman's face, it was pretty clear whining didn't go over big with her. "I told you," she said, annoyed, "those stories came to me. Through me. I didn't write them . . . and I can't write this."

"You *did* write them," I said. "It doesn't matter where the stories came from. Your words are what made Imaginalis come alive."

"Once," Mrs. Morice-Gilland said. "No more."

"If I could push past my limits . . . and, let's face it, I'm just some dumb twelve-year-old kid . . . then so can you."

"I'm old, Mehera," Mrs. Morice-Gilland said (and, all of a sudden, she sure sounded that way). "At the end of my life."

"Only if you believe it, right?" I answered. "I mean, thinking like that, isn't it just the prison of the possible? Just like in *Flight from Forever*, when—"

"Stop using my own words against me!" Mrs. M-G shouted. She slammed her hand against the top of the piano, her wedding picture falling off, crashing to the floor. There was glass everywhere. The old woman leaned her head into her hands—and I could see she was shaking. "I've lived a long life, Mehera. Long enough, anyway. Now if you want me to go back to Queenstown with you, do what I can to help Nossys and the others—"

"Prognostica said they had two, maybe three days. We can bring Prince Imagos back and *still* have time to—"

"Prognostica," the old woman said, "isn't the most dependable of oracles."

"Can't you at least try?" I pleaded. "I mean," I went on, pointing to Yalee, who was sitting there all quiet, just kind of studying the two of us, "you brought *him* here, all the way from Nolandia. If you can do *that*—"

"Nolandia is one thing, Mehera," Mrs. Morice-Gilland said. "Death is quite another."

"Why won't you even *try*?" I said, getting madder and madder. The old woman looked up—she was angry, too, now—then turned away.

Neither of us said a word for a minute or two. I knelt down, picked up the picture frame, shook out the broken glass, and set it back down on the piano. "I'll get a broom," I said.

"No," Mrs. Morice-Gilland said quietly. "Leave it. I'll clean it up later." She stared at the photo for a really long time, then turned to the winged lion. "Do *you* think I can do it?"

"Mehera is right," Yalee said. "However they came to

you, Dreamer, you wrote those books. You. Nobody else. You have a connection to our people, to our world, that no other soul in the ten million intersecting universes has."

"Except *her*," Mrs. M-G said, pointing to me—and I wasn't sure, but it sounded like maybe she was a little jealous of me. "I don't think there's anyone in any world who believes in Imaginalis as passionately as she does."

"If I do," I answered, "it's because of you."

"My Prince," the lion said, "believed that the two of you, together, can make miracles even Imaginalis has never seen."

Mrs. Morice-Gilland stood quietly, drumming her bent old fingers on the piano top, then said, "All right, I'll do it."

"That's fantastic!" I said.

"But that doesn't mean I'll succeed," Mrs. Morice-Gilland said.

"I know," I answered. "But at least, y'know, you'll have tried. And that has to count for something. Remember what Rajah Merogji said to Prince Imagos, in the very first Imaginalis book, when Imagos was afraid to enter that archery contest? 'Do your best, then leave the Silver Queen the rest'?"

"Shallow," Mrs. Morice-Gilland said. "Insipid. Corny beyond belief."

"And true," Yalee added.

"We'll see." Mrs. Morice-Gilland walked across the living room toward her office. She threw open the door, then turned and glared at me. *"Well?"* she asked.

"Well what?"

"Aren't you coming?"

"Don't you, y'know, need to be alone?"

"Didn't Yalee just say something about the two of us together?" She folded her arms across her chest, tapped her foot, and looked at me in a funny way. It was like she was seeing me . . . or maybe something *in* me . . . for the first time. I couldn't tell if that was a bad or a good thing, but at least she wasn't glaring anymore.

I rushed across the room—no way I was going to argue with her—and the two of us went into the office.

"Just sit there," Mrs. Morice-Gilland ordered me, pointing to an old easy chair in the corner.

"And do what?" I asked.

The old woman thought about that for a moment, then said: "You'll sit there . . . in *silence*, please . . . and think of Prince Imagos. See him in your mind's eye, alive and well, happy and healthy."

"I can do that."

"Let's hope so," the old woman mumbled. Mrs. Morice-Gilland slid out her desk chair, settled into it, rolled a sheet of paper into an old typewriter the size of a small car.

"You really should get a computer," I said.

"In *silence*."

"Yes, ma'am."

I settled in, stretching out in the chair. I closed my eyes, but (I couldn't help it) every few seconds I took a peek at Mrs. Morice-Gilland. Thing was, she was just sitting there, staring at the typewriter like she expected it to start typing on its own. She sighed. She fidgeted. She bit her lip. "I can't," she finally said.

And then . . . it felt like it wasn't even me doing it, like it was something inside me pushing me along . . . I got up and walked over to her. "Because it's impossible, I'll *do* it," I said.

Mrs. Morice-Gilland looked up at me—I thought she was going to yell at me or something, but she didn't— then back at the blank page. "Because it's unbelievable," she said, "I'll believe." Then the two of us started saying it together, kind of like we were *chanting* it, over and over and over—"Because it's impossible, I'll do it; because it's unbelievable, I'll believe!"—for maybe ten minutes until, at *the exact same moment*, we both stopped, like we knew the time was right. Like we knew exactly what we had to do.

And we did!

We started typing, writing everything we thought or felt, everything we remembered or imagined, about Prince Imagos. Banging away so hard, it was amazing the keys didn't crack and fall apart. That's right, I said *we* started typing. My hands were right next to Mrs. M-G's, our fingers flying across the keyboard together, like we were one of those four-armed Hindu gods in my mother's old India photographs. Four arms and one mind: She'd have a thought, and I'd write it. I'd start a sentence, and she'd finish it.

"We need more words, Mehera!" Mrs. Morice-Gilland shouted, our hands moving so fast I could hardly see them. "More wonderful, glorious words! Each letter is magic! Each combination of letters is a spell! Each sentence brings him closer to us!"

"Proud!" I shouted—and the word hit the paper.

"Compassionate!" she answered—and that appeared next.

"Powerful!"

"Wise!"

"Handsome!"

"Humble!"

"Loyal!"

"Fierce!"

"The greatest Prince," we shouted together, the typewriter keys pounding like drums, "that Imaginalis has ever known!"

Mrs. Morice-Gilland was laughing now, so hard, so loud, it was like she'd waiting twenty years to let it all out. And—I couldn't help it—I started laughing, too. We'd tear out one page, roll in another. Page after page after page—until the whole office was filled with paper, flying through the air, covering the floor. Until our fingers ached. Until we couldn't laugh anymore. Until the words finally stopped.

"Are we done?" I asked her.

"Spent," Mrs. Morice-Gilland said. She squeezed out one last giggle. "I don't think I've had that much fun in years." She leaned over, gathered up some of the pages. "But I don't think it worked, darling." I wasn't sure I heard right. Had she just called me darling? "I think we failed him."

"Just wait," I said.

"Wait for what?"

We heard an incredible roar—the most joyful roar in the History of Roaring—from the other room. "For *that!*" I squealed, grabbing Mrs. Morice-Gilland's hand and pulling her (maybe a little harder than you should pull an old lady) out of the office and into the living room—

Where a winged lion flew in circles around the Prince of Imaginalis.

"Prince Imagos!" I shrieked, throwing my arms around him and giving him a humongous squeeze.

"Indeed, Mehera," he said, squeezing back, grinning at me. "Indeed!"

"You did it!" I said, turning to Mrs. Morice-Gilland. I was so over-the-moon, super-deluxe delirious that I started dancing. *"You did it!"* Then—and you're *really* not going to believe this—Mrs. M-G started dancing, too.

"No, Mehera," she said. "We did it. *We* did it." And that started her crying. Good crying. Happy crying. "Idiot," she said, wiping her tears away with her sleeve. "Sentimentalist."

"A few tears of appreciation are quite appropriate, Dreamer," Imagos said as Yalee flew down to his side, "considering that you've just raised a prince from the dead! Now let's do the same for Imaginalis!"

CHAPTER TWENTY-SEVEN
Flying

Since Prince Imagos didn't think Mrs. Morice-Gilland could handle a slide through an astral tunnel—and, boy, was she relieved when he said that—he decided to let Yalee fly us back to Queenstown. But we couldn't all fit on Yalee's back, so, using another spell that Uncle Nossyss had taught him, the Prince enchanted an old Persian rug he found in Mrs. Morice-Gilland's basement and, no kidding, transformed it into a flying carpet. "Given a choice between a lion's back and a dusty carpet," Mrs. Morice-Gilland said, "I'll take the rug. No offense meant, Yalee," she added.

"None taken," the lion answered.

Mrs. M-G looked so peaceful, so happy—like she'd been flying on carpets her entire life. She tossed her head back and let the wind just kind of whip through her hair. Me, I guess I'd finally overcome my fear of heights, because I wasn't scared at all. We were all pretty wiped from everything we'd been through, and so we flew on, not saying anything for a long time. It may have been the nicest silence I've ever heard, if you know what I mean. After a while, I turned to Imagos. "Where were you?" I asked quietly. "Y'know, when you . . . died? Where did you go?"

The Prince thought about that for a long time. "I can't say. I will *never* say."

"Because you don't remember?"

"No, Mehera," Imagos said, "because I *do*."

"I don't understand."

Mrs. Morice-Gilland did. "Some things," she said, "are too sacred to be spoken." The Prince nodded. "One word of description," he said softly, "and I just might destroy it."

I wouldn't give up. I couldn't. I just had to know. "But there is . . . *someplace* that everyone goes?"

The Prince thought about that for a long time. "I don't know about *everyone*, Mehera," he finally said. "I only know about *me*." His eyes got all shiny. There were tears there, but they never fell. "But if I could make a guess, then . . . *yes*, I'd say everyone does go . . . well, not where I went, perhaps. But to someplace like it. Tailor-

233

made, just for them." A whisper. "Just for them."

All of a sudden I got scared, worried. And guilty. "Was it hard to come back? Did we do something wrong? Should we have left you there?"

"No, Mehera," Prince Imagos answered. "No. What you did was right. What you did was *perfect*." The little mindfire flew up, out of my vest pocket, circling around the Prince's head, its light reflecting off his crown. "I *love* life. It's the most wonderful gift there is. I love every breath and movement, every joy and sorrow, failure and triumph." He got this odd look on his face, like he wasn't looking out at the world anymore but inside himself. I could tell he was remembering where he'd been, what he'd experienced. "But when the day comes for me to return there, I won't offer any arguments. Not one word of protest."

He reached out and took my hand. I didn't even think about it, just slipped my fingers between his. It didn't feel weird at all. It just felt . . . right.

We were silent again, all the way home to Queenstown.

CHAPTER TWENTY-EIGHT
Shadows and Light

When we got back to the tree house, we rushed into Uncle Nossyss's room—but he wasn't there. We searched the whole place—there were dozens of rooms, and it took nearly an hour—but there was no trace of either the old elephant or Prognostica. At first I thought maybe the Nebulous Seer had found some cure for Uncle Nossyss and the two of them were out walking around the neighborhood or maybe waiting across the way in my house. "Or who knows?" I said, excited. "They might have even found their way back to Imaginalis and—"

"No," Mrs. Morice-Gilland said (and she sounded pretty sure of herself), "that's not it. They're gone."

"How do you know that?" I asked.

"I can *feel* it, Mehera," the old woman answered. "And

so can you." The truth is, I could. There was something *different* in the tree house now: a kind of emptiness. A kind of loneliness.

The lion growled softly. "Prognostica's prediction was wrong," he said. "Again." He held up a paw, I guess checking to see if the moonlight was passing through it. Not yet—but we all knew it was coming. Pretty soon Yalee would fade into Nolandia, and then Prince Imagos, too. What was the point of us saving him like that if—in another day or two, maybe another *hour*—he was just going to become . . . nothing.

I couldn't take any more. I sat down on the edge of the old elephant's bed and buried my face in my hands. "All this," I said. "All this . . . and we failed?" I'd cried enough tears for one day, but now there were more on the way.

"Is this," Prince Imagos asked the group, "what you have all chosen? Grief and surrender?"

"We haven't chosen anything," I whined. "This is the way things *are*, and there's nothing we can do about it."

Imagos sat down on the bed next to me. "All you've seen, Mehera, all you've accomplished . . . and you can still say that?" I was hoping maybe he'd hold my hand again, but he didn't. "Choose grief, Mehera, and you'll see only a *universe* of grief. But choose hope . . ." He looked at me, at Mrs. Morice-Gilland, at Yalee—and there was something in his face. Something *regal*, I guess. He didn't just look like a prince, he looked like a king. The Greatest King *Ever*. "And you'll see miracles."

Imagos pointed across the room. I looked—but nothing was different. There were a few mindfires flying around. Moonlight was coming in through the windows, and the shadows of the trees outside were waving across the walls. But then I saw that it wasn't just the trees: There were other shadows there, too. *Two* others—and they were moving like they were alive, sliding across the walls, up to the ceiling, then crawling down to the floor. They may have been just silhouettes, but I recognized them right away: "Prognostica!" I shouted, running across the room. "Uncle Nossyss!"

They were alive. Shadows now, almost gone—but *still alive*. I reached out to grab Prognostica's hand—but she slid away from me. I reached for the old elephant, and he did the same thing. "What's wrong with them?" I asked, turning to Imagos. "It's like they're afraid of me."

"They're in the final stages now," the Prince said, and that phrase—"final stages"—made me want to scream or cry or throw up (or maybe all three). "They don't remember us. I don't think they even remember themselves. They're just darkness and instinct. Confusion and fear."

"Then we *are* too late." I sighed.

Mrs. Morice-Gilland whapped me—not hard, just enough to get my attention—on the top of my head. "This is no time for self-pity. This," she went on, with a smile so big it pushed half the wrinkles off her face, "is the time to *build*."

"The Bridge?" I said.

"The Bridge."

And I knew that, together, we'd make the most unbelievable Unbelievable Bridge there ever was.

It was right there, shimmering, just outside the door, the deck of the Bridge touching the edge of the tree house, flooding every room with light.

We—Prince Imagos, Mrs. Morice-Gilland, Yalee, and I—stood there at the door, just staring at it . . . just *feeling* it . . . and, I couldn't help myself, I started crying *again*. But these were the most wonderful tears in the History of Crying. I could have cried like that forever. When I turned to look at the others, I noticed that they were crying, too. Even the winged lion.

"We must bring the shadows out," Prince Imagos said quietly.

"How?" I asked. "Every time we get near them, they—"

"I wasn't talking to *you*," he said.

Before I could say another word, something started jumping around in my vest pocket, and then the little mindfire shot straight up into the air and back into the tree house. Without thinking, I ran after it. It flew from room to room, chiming a song that sounded like a church hymn that had been sped up and played backward on a circus calliope. It was maybe the goofiest—and most beautiful—song I'd ever heard. Nossyss and Prognostica (no matter what they looked like, I couldn't think of them as just shadows) must have liked the music, too, because they started dancing to the tune, sliding down the walls, across the floors, and following the little mindfire out into the night.

I followed them out and noticed that Mrs. Morice-Gilland was staring at the sky. I looked, too: There were hundreds, maybe thousands, of stars up there. And more were showing up every second.

"I think the Dreamer should lead the way," Prince Imagos said.

Mrs. Morice-Gilland smiled and bowed her head. "It would be an honor," she said, "but only if Mehera walks beside me." She reached out her hand, I reached back, and together we stepped out onto the deck. The Prince and the lion, the chiming mindfire, and the two shadows were all walking behind us.

I looked back to see that the tree house had vanished—and so had my house, my neighborhood, my entire *world*. Up above us, the stars started to move, first in slow circles, then spinning faster and faster. Then, all at once, they started pouring out of the sky . . . it was like it was *raining stars* . . . gathering together on the walkway behind us. But they weren't stars anymore. They were animals and humans, tree spirits and ocean devas, mountain gods and cloud goddesses and so many more. The Imaginalians were free and ready to return home.

Home: It was there now, right ahead of us, at the end of that endless Bridge. I could see the towers and the Transpheres and the lights of the Rajah's palace, reflecting off Amaram Lake.

"A Golden Age, Mehera," a familiar voice said. "No war, no conflict. A new era of peace and abundance that even the Silver Queen would envy."

"Uncle Nossyss!" I squealed, throwing my arms around the old elephant (well, as far around as they'd go). "You're all right, you're all right, *you're all right*," I said. "And what about Prognostica?" I asked. "Is she—?"

"Right here, dear." The Nebulous Seer eased herself through the crowd. "I knew you'd save us," she said, her voice tinkling like a piano. "I saw it in a vision, before we ever met."

"Of course you did," Uncle Nossyss said. The old elephant wrapped his trunk around my shoulders. Kissed me on the top of my head. "I owe you my life, child," he said.

"As do I," Prince Imagos said. "My life—and the life of my kingdom." Uncle Nossyss backed away and the Prince lifted my chin, stared straight into my eyes. "You, Mehera Beatrice Crosby," he said, "are *my* hero."

"Thank you, Your Majesty." I looked back into those amazing brown eyes—and suddenly realized how much had changed since I gave that Imaginalis report in English. I didn't feel like some clumsy, awkward doofus anymore. No, I felt like . . . like Mehera Beatrice Crosby. And, all of a sudden, that seemed like the perfect person to be.

The Prince and his Companions gathered around me and Mrs. Morice-Gilland, while behind us, the people of Imaginalis stood in silence.

"Are you ready," Uncle Nossyss said, turning to Mrs. Morice-Gilland, "to begin your new life?"

"*My* new life?" The old woman looked toward the city in the distance. A city she'd written about so many times but had never really seen. "Are you saying that I . . . I can go with you? *Stay* with you?"

"You are the Dreamer," Prince Imagos said, bowing his head, touching his heart, "and it would be an honor to have you living with us in the royal palace."

She just looked at the Prince for the longest time and finally said, "It would be a wonderful place to spend my last days."

"Last days?" Uncle Nossyss said. "In Imaginalis, a single day is nearly a century, so I can promise you a very long and very happy life. Perhaps you won't live forever. . . ." He waved his hand over the old woman's head and, just like that, the age spots disappeared from Mrs. Morice-Gilland's skin, her white hair turned black, every single wrinkle vanished—and she looked *exactly* like the woman in the wedding picture on her piano. "But I suspect it will be close enough."

"*Look* at me, Mehera," Mrs. Morice-Gilland said, turning to me.

I started bawling again. "You're beautiful," I said. "But the truth is, Mrs. Morice-Gilland, you were just as beautiful before."

"Call me Mikela." Mrs. M-G folded me in her arms and held me tight. "Thank you for finding me, Mehera," she said.

I couldn't stop crying and, honestly, I didn't want to. "And thank you," I said, "for every word you've ever written. And every word to come." I grinned at her. "I don't think you're gonna have any problems coming up with stories now, Mrs. Mo— Uh . . . Mikela."

"And so, Mehera," Prince Imagos announced, "it's

time for us to go. You know, of course, that you're welcome to come with us. To stay in Imaginalis for as long as you'd like."

"Thank you, Prince Imagos," I said. "And I promise that I *will* come one day. But right now . . . right now I have to go back." I corrected myself. "No, I don't *have* to go. I *want* to go. More than I've ever wanted anything before."

Imagos didn't seem surprised in the least, but he still had to ask. "Why?"

"Because," I answered, "from now on, I'm going to choose. Every day I'm going to choose love—more and more. See the king instead of his pockets. Who knows? Maybe *we'll* have a Golden Age, too."

"Impossible," the Prince said.

"Exactly," I answered.

The Prince leaned forward and gave me the softest, sweetest kiss (on the cheek! Hey, I'm only twelve, you know). "Good-bye, Mehera," he said. "For now."

The winged lion padded up to me and licked my face. I ran my hands through his mane, took a sniff of that wonderful sweet breath, and told him that, from then on, he'd always be one of my very favorite characters.

Uncle Nossyss stepped forward, touched my face with his trunk, fighting back a few tears of his own. "What is there to say?" he whispered. And he was right. When two people know each other the way we do, words just get in the way.

Finally I turned to say good-bye to Prognostica, but the Nebulous Seer was off in a trance, humming a weird tune, arms snaking and fingers spidering. Gazing ahead into a hundred could be/maybe futures.

"What did you see?" I asked when her vision had passed.

"A time when you return to us," Prognostica answered, and she sounded more certain than I'd ever heard her. "An extraordinary young woman . . . of extraordinary gifts . . . married to our beloved Prince. Ruling beside him as an equal, Queen of all Imaginalis." I looked over at the Prince; he looked over at me. I think maybe he was blushing. I know I sure was.

"Wait," Uncle Nossyss said.

"Or," Prognostica added, with a smile in her voice, "maybe not."

Crying *and* laughing now, I gave the Nebulous Seer a humongoid hug; then I waved good-bye to the Companions and headed back across the Unbelievable Bridge.

Into the hope of night.

EPILOGUE
Another Ending, Another Beginning

"Mehera!" my father shouted when I walked into the living room. "Mehera, it's *eleven o'clock!* Where have you *been?*"

I stood there for a couple of seconds, just gawping at him—not because Papa was angry, but because I suddenly remembered that awful image Pralaya had shown me: Papa, white as a sheet, wheezing and gasping, on the floor of A Thousand Voices.

"I got home from the store," Papa said, "and there was no note, no message on the answering machine. I've been sitting here for hours, worried sick, calling your friends and—" He noticed that I was looking at him kind of funny. "Don't just stand there staring at me, Mehera Bea," he went on. "You've never done anything like this before, and I want an explanation."

I raced into his arms, knocking him back onto the couch, kissing him on his forehead and cheeks over and over. *"Papa!"* I squealed. "Papa, *promise* me you'll live to be a hundred!"

He gave me this look like he was totally worried, or maybe totally delighted. Or maybe both. "What's this all about, goose?"

"Look," I said, the words rushing out so fast it was amazing they made any sense, "I'm *really, really* sorry that I didn't call and I *swear* that it will never happen again . . . well, maybe it will but not till I'm at *least* sixteen . . . and *please*, Papa, if you just don't ask me where I was, I promise that one day I'll tell you, even if you're never gonna believe it, not in a million years."

"Nothing bad happened, did it?" Papa asked. I could tell he was getting ready to call the president.

"No, no, nothing bad happened, and I'm perfectly fine. I'm fantastic. I *swear* I am."

"Okay," he said, surprising me. And himself, too, I think.

"Okay?"

I know he could have pushed it, could have yelled at me, sent me to my room, cut off my internet for a week, taken away my cell phone, but I could tell that something inside Papa—maybe it was some personal magic of his own—was holding him back. Telling him it was all right to trust me. "Okay," he said again.

"Thanks, Papa," I said, snuggling in close. "And I *promise* that it won't—" I stopped, noticing a stack of what looked like travel brochures on the coffee table. "What's that?" I asked.

"Oh, that," Papa said, grabbing the brochures away from me. "I didn't really want you to see those, goose. At least not till—"

"Hand 'em over," I said, grabbing them back.

"Mehera, listen, this is nothing definite. I was just thinking that maybe this summer . . . y'know, after school lets out . . . maybe we could take a trip together and—"

"*India?*" I yelped. "Guided tours of *India?*"

"You *bet* guided tours," Papa answered. "Air-conditioned buses, first-class hotels, none of that pooping in holes this time, not for me."

"*India?*" I yelped again. "But you swore you'd never go there again."

Papa shrugged. "Hey," he said, "a guy can't spend *every* minute with his nose in a book. 'Life itself is the most wonderful fairy tale,' right?"

"Right."

"So let's live it, goose," Papa said, kissing me on the